Tales from Around the World

NEW YORK

Cover illustration by Lyn Cawley

Cover design by Kasa and Steel

First published in USA 1987 by Exeter Books
Distributed by Bookthrift
Exeter is a trademark of Bookthrift Marketing, Inc.
Bookthrift is a registered trademark of
Bookthrift Marketing, Inc.
New York, New York.

ISBN 0-671-08502-6

Printed in Hong Kong by Dai Nippon

CONTENTS

The Man Who Knew Better.

A man once said to his wife, "I don't know what you find to do all day. You only have to tidy up, watch the baby and cook a bite to eat."

"Oh, there's the cow and the pig to look after, and the butter to churn," said his wife.

But her husband snorted, "Hah! that's nothing. I'm the only person in this house who does any work — out in the fields in the hot sun. I wish I was a housewife and could stay home all day!"

"Well, why not have a rest, tomorrow?" said his wife, smiling sweetly. "I'll go and cut the corn, and you can do my few jobs around the house."

The man grinned the smuggest of grins. "An excellent idea! Then I can show you how a house *should* be kept — and you'll realise how hard I work!"

So, next morning, before the sun was up, the wife had taken the scythe and gone into the fields to cut corn.

"First I'll churn some butter," said the man, and he filled the churn in the kitchen with fresh cream.

Then he thought how good a mug of cider would taste. So he went down to the cellar, set a jug under the barrel, and turned on the tap.

Suddenly he remembered the pig! Forgetting the cider, he raced upstairs again.

Suddenly he remembered the cider! Forgetting the baby, he raced downstairs again.

Too late! Every drop of cider had emptied itself out across the cellar floor. He had to mop it all up and empty it on to the vegetable garden. "While I'm here," he thought, "I'll pick some vegetables for the soup."

Suddenly he remembered the baby! Forgetting the vegetables and the open gate, he raced indoors again.

Too late! The baby had climbed up the milk churn and tipped it over. There was cream on the floor. There was cream on the baby. There was cream everywhere. He mopped it up, and put the baby in the sun to dry.

Too late! The pig had wandered in through the open back door and tipped over the churn. He had to drive out the pig, wipe up the mess and fill the churn all over again. The baby gurgled and crawled around his feet.

That was when he saw the cow looking all hungry and woe-begone. "I must feed her, but I haven't time to take her up to the meadow," he thought. "I know. I'll put her up on the roof. There's plenty of grass on the thatch."

Now the roof reached almost down to the ground, so with a bit of pushing and pulling, he managed to get the cow on to the roof. And once she was up, she was happy to eat the grass that grew on the thatch.

Suddenly he remembered the open gate! Forgetting the cow and the creamy baby, he raced down to the vegetable garden.

Too late! The pig had got in already and eaten every vegetable in it. He had to drive her out and set about mending all the beanpoles.

Suddenly he remembered the cow! Supposing she had fallen off the roof on to the baby while his back was turned? Dropping everything, he raced back to the house.

But, no, the cow was still up on the roof, chewing on the grass. But to make her even safer, he tied a rope round her neck, dropped the end down the chimney, went down to the kitchen and tied the other end of the rope round his waist.

"That'll keep her safe while I make the soup," he thought, and set a cooking pot of water over the fire.

Suddenly, the cow fell off the roof.

Down went the cow on one end of the rope. Up went the man on the other end. He flew up the chimney like a squirrel up a tree and wedged near the top.

Not long afterwards, his wife came home. "I'm back, dear! The corn's all cut.

the rope — *splash* — into the cooking pot. His wife found him sitting there, with a carrot in his ear, wailing, "Oh! What a day I've had! What a day!"

"Never mind," said his wife. "You may have better luck tomorrow —

Where are you? Dear!"

She found the baby sitting in the sun — all stiff and spikey where the cream had dried. She found the empty garden. She found the cow dangling from the roof. "Dear, dear, what has your father been doing?" she said to the baby as she cut the rope with her scythe.

Down came the cow on her end of the rope, with a bellow of indignation. Down came the husband on his end of

although there's the washing to do, and fresh bread to bake. Myself, I think I'll mow the top meadow, tomorrow."

"Oh no you don't!" cried her husband leaping out of the cooking pot. "I mean . . . I wouldn't *dream* of letting you do all that work. You stay home tomorrow — *I'll* mow the meadow."

"Very well, dear," said his wife, smiling to herself as she started to prepare dinner. "Whatever you say."

THE MIGHTY PRINCE

Long ago, in Japan, there lived a great Prince. He was rich and powerful, and his people were good and loyal. Yet the Prince was an unhappy man.

He was short-tempered and impatient. He was always angry and often cruel. He bullied his subjects until they cringed with fear.

One year he waged war on a neighbouring country. At his word of command his troops hurled themselves into battle, their spears thrust out before them, their cruel Prince behind. They fought bravely and won a great victory for him, but still he was not satisfied. Still he was unhappy.

The army returned home with the victorious Prince at their head. Day after day wonderful victory parades were held, and at night the skies glowed with fireworks and lanterns as the people praised their Prince and celebrated his great deeds.

But the people soon grew sad. The Prince noticed their long faces, and he blazed with anger.

"Speak!" he roared as he rode through the streets on his great war-horse. "Why are you so sorrowful?"

His subjects bowed low but no-one had the courage to tell him the truth — that they were tired of war, tired of victories. So they stayed silent.

Later that day, as he rode slowly through the countryside, he heard a soft humming, like a shower of rain on dry ground. The Prince stopped and listened. He looked around and listened again.

It was a little girl singing as she worked in her small garden. So busy was she, planting her seeds, that she did not realise the great Prince was standing behind her.

At first he was angry that she did not notice him. Why should he, a proud and mighty Prince, humbly beg for her attention? But something in her singing made him wait quietly. After some time, he coughed and shuffled his feet.

The little girl slowly turned her head and saw the Prince in his rich, silk robes.

The Prince looked down at her and met her clear, calm gaze, and felt his anger at the people's silence melting away.

The child rose to her feet. Bowing humbly, she offered the Prince a bag of seed. For a moment he felt offended that one of his subjects should offer him such a humble gift, but then he found himself taking the bag. He did not say "thank you", or even smile, but turned away from the little girl. The mighty Prince felt

looked at it, tears rolled down his face, because he could not understand why Spring made everyone happy. Everyone, that is, except him.

He never had understood, of course, but this year he cried because he had worked so hard to create a beautiful garden and he wanted so much to know the secret of happiness.

Then, quietly, he seemed to hear the soft voice of the little girl speaking to him. It was telling him to look — to look with all his heart at the flowers and the grass, the sky and the birds, the busy insects and all the laughing people.

And suddenly the Prince saw them all as he had never done before. A great joy flooded his heart, and he saw the colours sparkling in the sun and he smelled the scent of a million flowers. And for the very first time, he felt happiness and a real love for his people.

puzzled as he rode slowly back to his palace, and that night he slept with the bag of seed by his pillow.

The next morning he woke full of strength and energy, as if he were ready for war. But there was to be no war today. No, today the Prince had very different plans.

"Planting is no work for princes," he mumbled as he took up the bag of seed. "But it is better than fighting people who do not know how to fight back."

The people were astonished to see the Prince working in the palace gardens. And day after day, week after week, month after month, he tended his plants. Through heat and cold, he laboured over his task.

Then, one morning, Spring suddenly arrived! The garden burst into flower and fragrance. Bees and birds hummed. The people gathered in the streets, smiling in the sunshine. But where was the Prince? He had worked so hard to create the garden, why was he not rejoicing in it with his people?

The Prince stood apart, holding in his hand a spray of blossom. And as he

QUEST OF THE BRAVE

The other indian braves laughed at Scarface. They laughed at him because he was so poor. They laughed at him, too, because of the ugly scar that spoiled his face.

"Why don't you ask Brightgirl to marry you, Scarface?" they mocked. "She's refused the richest, best-looking braves from seven villages. How could she resist *you* with all your money and that face!"

They knew how much their jokes hurt Scarface. He loved Brightgirl. To their great surprise Scarface said, "I *shall* go and ask her, for it is not always wealth or a good face that wins a woman's heart." The young men laughed even louder, but at noon Scarface walked down to the river to find the squaw called Brightgirl.

"I tell you honestly," he began,

"I have no family, no wealth, and you can see for yourself the face I have. But if you care at all about the love in my heart . . . marry me."

Brightgirl stared at him. She did not seem frightened by the scar, and she did not laugh at him.

At last she said, "The Sun spoke to me when I was young. He said, 'Never marry, for you are mine!' That is why I refuse all the young men who ask for my hand. But never until now have I found it hard. I don't know why, but if it were not for my promise to the Sun, I would marry you, Scarface, and be happy for ever."

berries and walked on, day after day. And just when he thought he could go no farther, he met Skunk. "I'm looking for the Sun's lodge," he told Skunk.

"In all my travels, I've never seen it," said Skunk. "But Bear is wise. Why not ask Bear?" So Scarface asked Bear.

"Oh!" cried Scarface. "If you had laughed at me, it would have been easier to bear! I'd like to take the Sun and shake him till he lets you go!"

"Shshsh! He might hear you!" Brightgirl glanced up at the Sun. "Scarface, if you love me, go to the Sun's lodge and ask him to free me. If his answer is yes, let him touch your face and mend it. Then everyone will know that he has given permission for us to marry."

His heart pounding, Scarface turned his back on the village and set off on his long, long search for the Sun.

He walked until all the food he had was gone. Then he lived on roots and

but he was half-dead with hunger and weariness before he saw his shadowy shape among the trees. And Wolverine told him bad news.

"The Sun's lodge is on the other side of the Great Water. Where is your canoe? How will you cross over?" Then, beyond the trees, Scarface glimpsed the wide,

"In all my travels, I've never seen the Sun's lodge. But Badger might know. Why not ask Badger!" So Scarface asked Badger.

"In all my travels, I've never seen the Sun's lodge. Why not ask Wolverine?" So Scarface looked for Wolverine,

wide sea, which he had never seen before. It stretched far, far away, farther than even his sharp eyes could see.

He sat down on the shore and wept, unable to go on, unable to turn back. And when two eagles flew overhead, he told them his sad, sad story. "Now I shall never reach the Sun's lodge, because it's on the other side of the wide, wide sea!"

The eagles swooped down and picked up Scarface and carried him across the ocean to the farthest shore. "There you are, young man," said one. "Because of your sad, sad story, we pity you. Follow that path and you will find the Sun's lodge."

Come and shelter for the night in my father's lodge."

Scarface bit his lip. "I would do, but I really must go on till I reach the Sun's lodge."

The handsome brave laughed out loud. "Of course — you don't know me! I am Morning Star, son of the great Sun."

So Scarface reached the Sun's lodge — and stayed not just for a night, but for many, many days. But when he was summoned to meet the Sun he felt too shy to mention his love for Brightgirl.

"My son likes you," said the Sun one morning. "Stay and be his friend. But don't let him play near the Lake of Birds. The Spike-bill birds peck men to death if they can!"

Scarface walked quickly up the steep, crumbling pathway. Scattered along the path he saw coats of the finest buffalo hide — arrows with shafts of gold, moccasins sewn with a coloured thread and a head-dress made from the plumes of every bird in the sky.

"He is rich indeed who owns these things," thought Scarface, but he did not touch them.

"Halt!" Out of a tree sprang a warrior, his hair braided and his face painted to look fierce, though he was hardly more than a boy. "Why did you not pick up the coats or the arrows or the moccasins or head-dress?" he asked.

"Because they are not mine!"

The warrior's painted face broke into a smile. "I see you are an honest man.

Outside the hut, Morning Star whispered to Scarface, "Take no notice. I *want* to go to the lake. I'll cut the heads off those silly birds!" And he ran ahead of Scarface who chased him calling, "Stop! Come back! It's dangerous!"

The Spike-bill birds looked harmless in the water, but as Morning Star ran down to the shore, they rose up like a raincloud over his head and plunged at him, their sharp beaks stabbing and scratching.

Scarface rushed forward, plunging in among the birds and scattering them. One by one they flapped away across the lake. Gently, Scarface carried Morning Star back to the lodge.

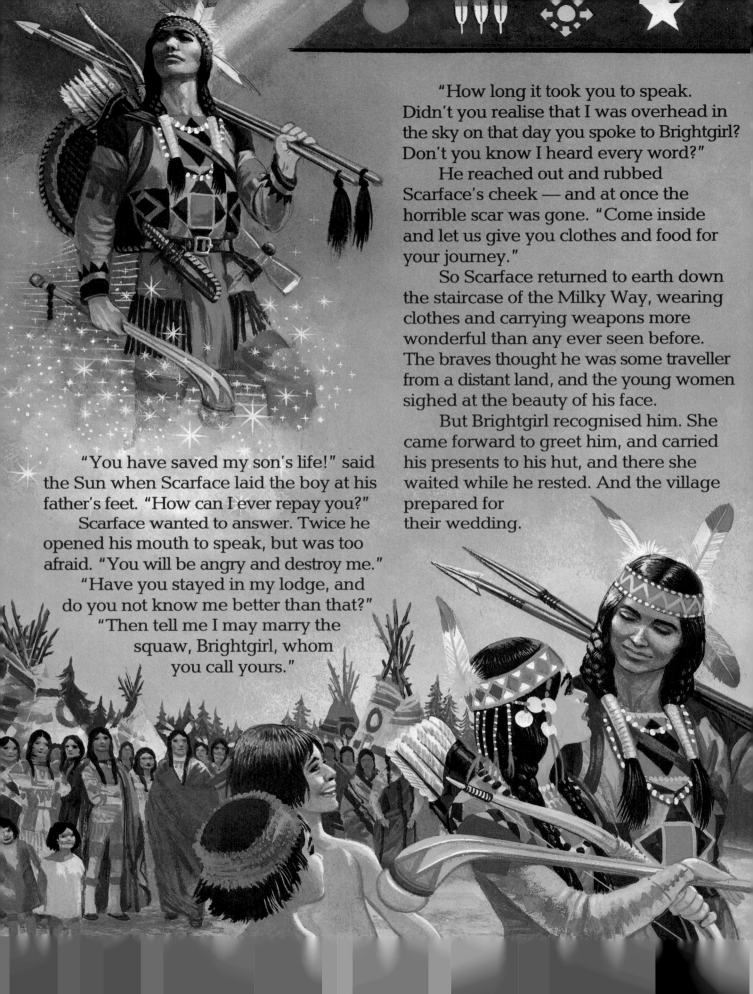

"How long it took you to speak. Didn't you realise that I was overhead in the sky on that day you spoke to Brightgirl? Don't you know I heard every word?"

He reached out and rubbed Scarface's cheek — and at once the horrible scar was gone. "Come inside and let us give you clothes and food for your journey."

So Scarface returned to earth down the staircase of the Milky Way, wearing clothes and carrying weapons more wonderful than any ever seen before. The braves thought he was some traveller from a distant land, and the young women sighed at the beauty of his face.

But Brightgirl recognised him. She came forward to greet him, and carried his presents to his hut, and there she waited while he rested. And the village prepared for their wedding.

"You have saved my son's life!" said the Sun when Scarface laid the boy at his father's feet. "How can I ever repay you?"

Scarface wanted to answer. Twice he opened his mouth to speak, but was too afraid. "You will be angry and destroy me."

"Have you stayed in my lodge, and do you not know me better than that?"

"Then tell me I may marry the squaw, Brightgirl, whom you call yours."

THE INN OF DONKEYS

Old Chao, the merchant, had travelled all over China and thought he knew all the inns and hotels in the country. One day, however, he found himself in a strange district and stopped to ask a farmer where he could find the nearest inn.

"Just over the hill," the farmer told him, "you'll find a very comfortable inn, and you can even buy donkeys there."

"Really!" exclaimed Chao. "I must say, it's time I bought a new beast. My old donkey is growing rather tired. Where do the donkeys come from?"

The farmer looked worried and said, "Well, I, I don't know. You can ask Third Lady, the innkeeper." Chao thanked the man, and rode on over the hill. At last he saw the Wooden Bridge Inn. Getting off his donkey, he went inside the inn.

Third Lady greeted him warmly. "I'm afraid I have no servants and must ask you to take your donkey to the stables yourself. But I'll prepare a meal and a bed for you."

That night Chao sat down with the six other guests to a delicious meal. Third Lady brought bottles of wine to the table. The six guests drank a great deal before falling wearily into their beds. But Chao did not drink any of the wine, and lay wide awake on his clean, soft bed. Just as he was dozing off, he was woken by the sound of a heavy thump. Fearing burglars were breaking into the inn, he peeped through a gap in the bamboo partition.

To his surprise he saw Third Lady dragging a heavy trunk across the earthen floor. He watched as she took some little carved figures from the trunk. Then she placed them on the floor. There was a man, an ox and a plough.

Third Lady hitched the plough behind the ox, and set the man behind the plough. Then she sprinkled some water over them and murmured some magic words. To Chao's astonishment, the little team began to move rapidly around the room!

In no time at all, the earthen floor

had been ploughed into neat furrows. Third Lady then placed a tiny basket of seeds into the wooden man's hand. No sooner had he planted the seeds, than fresh shoots of wheat appeared. Chao watched amazed as Third Lady gathered up the wheat, crushed it into flour and made little wheat cakes from the flour.

Chao was so troubled by this magic that he could not sleep. At last, as the sun peeped into his room, he packed his things. But just as he was about to leave the inn, Third Lady greeted him. "I have some delicious wheat cakes for your breakfast," she said. "Won't you stay?"

"Why, thank you," said Chao. "Do you mind if I just take one with me? I'm in a great hurry." He slipped the cake into his pocket and went to the stable to get his donkey. But he thought he would take just one more look at Third Lady, before setting off.

Peeping through the window, he saw her offering the little wheat cakes to the other guests. He watched them eat.

In amazement, he saw them roll upon the floor. Their clothes changed into rough grey fur; they grew long tails and big ears. Chao could not believe his eyes. The room was filled not with men, but with donkeys! Leaping on to his donkey, he scuttled away from the inn as fast as he could.

Chao did not stop until he reached the nearest city. And although his work kept him busy, he could not forget Third Lady and her strange and terrible magic.

When he had to leave the city, Chao bought six little cakes made of wheat. Packing these into one bag and the cake he had taken from Third Lady in another, he set off. He took the same road home as before, and once again stopped at the Wooden Bridge Inn.

Again, Third Lady gave him a warm welcome. And again when Chao got up in the morning, Third

Lady offered him some wheat cakes.

"Ah," said Chao, "I thought I would bring *you* some wheat cakes — do have one of mine."

With a scowl on her face, Third Lady took the cake Chao handed her. But the cake Third Lady took was the one she had given Chao on his first visit! No sooner had she eaten half, than she rolled upon the floor and turned into a donkey.

Chao was delighted. He pushed Third Lady out of the kitchen and tethered her to a tree. Then he hurried back to the inn and went to her bedroom and opened the trunk. Taking out the wooden toys, he burnt the little carved man, the ox and the plough.

And from that day on, until the end of his life, Third Lady proved to be a good, strong donkey and gave Chao very good service on his long travels through China.

SEADNA *and the* DEVIL

There was once a shoemaker whose name was Seadna. He lived by himself in a little cottage in the very middle of Ireland. He was a great man for eating and drinking and playing cards. Not a wake or a wedding for five miles around but there you would find Seadna, sitting in the chimney corner with a pipe

in his mouth and a glass in his hand.

As he was walking home late one night, a stranger spoke to him.

"You're out late, Seadna," said the stranger.

"And if I am," said Seadna, "what's that to you?"

"I've had my eye on you for a long time," said the stranger. "How would you like to have all the money you wanted for a whole year with never a worry about where it came from?"

"I wouldn't object at all," said Seadna.

"Well," said the stranger, "I'll give you all the money you want for a whole year and three wishes besides, if you'll come along with me at the end of that time. For I am the Devil," said he, "and you're the sort of man I want in my company."

Well, Seadna had no objection to the Devil's plan, for he was a crafty fellow and no spirit was going to get the better of him.

"It's a bargain," he said. "Now let me name my wishes."

"Name them," said the Devil, "and they're yours."

"I have a little stool," said Seadna, "and my first wish is that whoever sits on that stool will stick there till I release him."

"I grant your wish," said the Devil.

"Now here's my second wish," said Seadna. "I have an apple tree, and I wish that whoever plucks an apple from that tree will stick there till I release him."

"I grant your wish," said the Devil.

"And here's my third wish," said Seadna. "I have a leather purse, and I wish that whoever puts his hand in that purse will stick there till I release him."

"I grant your wish," said the Devil.

So the bargain was completed. The Devil shook hands with the shoemaker and walked away into the night.

The next day, Seadna found that his pockets were full of money, and every day for a whole year he never lacked gold or silver. Time passed so quickly that he hardly realised the year was up, until he heard the Devil's voice at the door one morning.

"Hurry up and prepare for the road!"

"Sit down there for a minute till I put on a collar and tie," said Seadna.

The Devil sat down on the stool.

"I'm ready now," said the shoemaker, when he had put on his collar and tie. So the Devil went to leave. But he could not get up — he was stuck fast to the stool.

"Free me from this stool!"

"If I do, will you give me another year of our bargain?" said Seadna.

"Oh, I will if I must," hissed the Devil. "I'll get you in the end anyway!" So Seadna released the Devil from the stool and let him get back to where he had come from.

The second year passed as quickly as the first, and one morning Seadna looked up to see the Devil standing in the doorway. "Ah, come in for a minute," said the shoemaker.

"I will not," said the Devil. "I had enough of that game last year! Come out now and let's be off!"

So Seadna came out of the cottage and they walked to the gate. As they passed the apple tree in the garden, Seadna raised up his hand and plucked a fistful of apples.

"These'll keep the thirst away while I'm walking," he said.

"Could I pick one too?" said the Devil greedily.

"And why not?" said Seadna. "I have no more use for them anyway."

The Devil raised up his hand to pluck an apple. His hand stuck fast to the tree.

"Free me from this tree!" yelled the Devil.

"If I do, will you give me another year of our bargain?" said Seadna.

"I will if I must," said the Devil. "I'll get you in the end anyway!" So Seadna released the Devil from the apple tree and let him go back to where he had come from.

The third year passed as quickly as the others, and early one morning Seadna heard the Devil's voice at the door, telling him to prepare for the road.

As soon as he was ready, he set off with the Devil and they walked side by side until they reached a town. There was an inn by the side of the road.

"I've a gold piece left in my pocket that belongs to you," said Seadna. "Would you like to have one drink for the road before we leave the town?"

"Well, yes," said the Devil, "but I don't know about going into an inn. People might laugh at my hooves and tail."

"Not at all. Can't you make yourself any shape you like? Can't you make yourself small enough to jump into my leather purse? Then I'll bring you inside myself and hand the drink to you."

"All right," said the Devil, and jumped into the purse. But he stuck fast there.

"Free me from this purse and I'll give you another year of our bargain," screeched the Devil.

"I will not," said the shoemaker. "I think we've had enough of that game."

And he took the purse down to the blacksmith's and laid it on the anvil.

"Take your hammer to that," said he to the smith, "and we'll give that lad a lesson he won't forget in a hurry."

So the blacksmith hammered away at the purse and the Devil roared within.

As for Seadna, he walked back to his cottage in the middle of Ireland. And he never heard from the Devil again.

Never tangle with a TENGU

As you probably know, nobody with any sense ever tangles with a tengu. But Iso San had so little brain that he once played a trick on one.

He had spent the morning trying to make a pea-shooter out of a length of bamboo. But the pea had got stuck down the tube. Iso San put the bamboo to his eye and tried to see the pea.

"Let me see through your telescope!" said a voice. And there beside him stood a smart little Japanese goblin — a tengu. Its nose was as curly as a pig's tail, and it wore wooden-heeled sandals, a cone-shaped shiny hat, and a wonderfully woven rice-straw coat. "Let me see, let me see!" squeaked the tengu, but Iso San shook his head.

"Oh no. The things I can see through here are far too wonderful."

"I'll give you my shiny hat if you let me look," said the tengu, trying to snatch the bamboo out of Iso's hand.

"Oh no. Why, I can see from Honshu to Hokkaido through this telescope!"

"Let me see!" squealed the tengu, "I'll give you my sandals!" But Iso San shook his head and held the pipe high out of reach. "I'll give you my invisible-making rice-straw coat!"

That was what Iso had been waiting for. "Agreed!" he exclaimed, and throwing down the pipe, he pulled the coat round his shoulders and ran off. When he looked back, the tengu was

trying to peer down the blocked pea-shooter. Steam was beginning to pour from its ears.

The moment Iso San buttoned up the rice-straw coat, he disappeared altogether. "What a joke!" he crowed, and hurried into town.

The people in the crowded streets could not see so much as a whisker of Iso San. So he boxed the ears of a big fat samurai. The samurai gasped and gaped and swung round with his fists up. And when he saw nobody there, he stepped backwards in astonishment. The invisible Iso was crouching behind him, ready to trip him up and send him sprawling in the mud!

After that, Iso San snatched the parasol out of a pretty girl's hand and raced through the streets with it

while the girl ran behind, crying, "Gracious! Oh! And not a puff of wind!"

A merchant who had just bought himself a new kimono stopped outside the shop to unwrap and admire it — only to see it fly off down the street!

The customers at the fish-shop were amazed to see a big fat bream leap off the slab and fly towards the river!

Iso San threw the parasol and the kimono off the bridge, but he carried the bream home for tea, tucked inside his magic coat. When he took off the coat, and hung it behind the door, he scared his old mother half to death. "Iso! Where did you spring from?" she gasped as he slapped the fish down on the table.

Iso San swaggered about. "Oh nowhere much — I've just been tangling with a tengu or two. Cook that for supper, will you, mother?" But he did not tell his mother about the rice-straw coat — or its magic.

the magic coat. "And I was going to go to the sake-house for a free drink! Oh, how could you?" Then an idea came to him. He took off all his clothes and smothered himself in the ashes of the burned coat.

Turning to his mother he said, "There now, how do I look?"

"Where *are* you?" said his mother.

"Excellent!" exclaimed the invisible Iso. "I'm off to the sake-house."

When he got there, he crept in and sat on the floor beside a barrel of sake. Without a sound, he turned the tap of the barrel and put his mouth under it to catch the trickle of wine. "This is the life!" he thought. Soon he had downed more sake than he had ever drunk in his life before.

Just then, the landlord's dog sniffed its way over to Iso San. "Push off!"

After Iso San had gone to bed, she took it down off the hook and shook it. "Dirty old thing," she muttered — and put it on the fire.

"You did *what*?" yelled Iso San next morning. He rushed to the fire and stared at the heap of ashes — all that was left of hissed Iso. "Go on — push off!"

At the sound of his voice, the dog grinned and panted and stared.

"Here, have a drop of this and then . . . hic . . . push off," whispered Iso San, cupping his hands under the tap and giving the dog a drink of sake.

The dog's tail began to wag. The sake was so delicious that the animal instantly loved Iso and started licking his face.

There was a noise of scraping chair legs. Iso San looked around. Everyone in the inn was staring at him, their faces white with fright. "What is it?" someone whispered. "A head with no body? Hands with no arms?"

Iso looked down at his hands. All the ash had been washed off with the wine, and the dog had licked his face clean. He was so shaken that he let sake trickle from the tap on to his feet.

"Agh! Feet without legs!" shrieked the landlord. "What will it be when it's finished appearing?"

"The devil itself!" shouted the customers, and picking up their chairs they threw them at Iso San. Then they chased him outside with brooms and swords and bottles.

"It's only me! It's *me*!" squealed Iso. But all the people could see was a face and a pair of hands and feet.

"Out! Out! No devils here!" they shouted, and Iso had to run with all his might under the hot, midday sun.

Sweat sprang from his skin, and as the rice-straw ash became damp, its magic disappeared — and there was another patch of Iso showing. Soon he looked like a half-finished drawing, as he fled towards the river with the whole town after him.

At the bridge, he dived off the road and into the water where the last of the ash washed off and floated away, leaving Iso stark naked and *very* cold. The townspeople hung over the bridge pelting him with rocks. "Look, it's me! It's *me*!" wailed Iso.

"Iso San! What *have* you been up to?" demanded the landlord.

They would not let Iso out of the water until he had explained everything. "P-please won't somebody f-f-fetch me something to wear?" he grizzled, shivering in the shallows.

"Not unless you promise to pay for all you drank," called the landlord.

"And to buy me a new kimono!" roared the merchant.

"And to buy me a new parasol!" squeaked the young girl.

"And to pay for my fish!" yelled the fishmonger.

"And not until I've boxed your ears!" shouted the samurai.

From the shadows of the bridge, a mischievous little face looked out. A goblin, dressed in a shiny, conical hat and wooden-heeled sandals, grinned at Iso. "Now you know why you should never tangle with a tengu," it said . . . and then pinged him with his own pea-shooter.

The Magic Porridge Pot

"Would you look after something for me?"

"Of course I will," said Maisie.

The witch threw open her cloak to reveal a little iron pot with three legs and a handle. "Take good care of it until I come back . . . Oh, and Maisie, if you should ever be hungry, just say to the pot 'Boil, pot, boil!' And if it should ever be full, just say the words 'Stop, pot, stop!' Can you remember?"

Maisie was just wondering how the witch knew her name when a gust of wind stirred up all the fallen leaves in a flurry. When they settled, the witch had disappeared.

One summer, long ago, the harvest failed and there was too little food to eat. In one house, in one particular village, there was no food at all.

Maisie lived there with her mother. Each day Maisie went into the wood to pick berries for supper. But winter was coming, and one day there were no berries to be found. Maisie sat down on a log, and a tear rolled down her cheek. "Whatever will become of mother and me?"

"I think you're just the person I'm looking for," said a gentle, crackly voice. There stood a crooked witch, wrapped in a bulging cloak, with only her purple face peeping out. "I'm travelling far away, and I can't carry much luggage," said the witch.

Lunchtime came, and Maisie's mother began to feel hungry. She took out the pot and looked at it greedily. "Boil, pot, boil!" she said, and at once the iron pot filled to the brim with porridge. "That's enough, thank you very much."

But the pot went on boiling. It went on boiling until it had spilled all over the table. "Oh dear! Halt, pot, halt!" But the little pot kept making porridge until the kitchen floor was covered. Maisie's mother climbed on to a chair.

Maisie walked home and set the pot on the kitchen table. "Look, Mother. We must take great care of this. I *think* it might be magic!"

"But where are the berries for supper?" asked her mother. "I'm hungry."

"So am I," thought Maisie, so she said aloud, "Boil, pot, boil!"

With a deliciously oozing, bubbling, simmering sound, the little pot filled to the brim with golden porridge laced with treacle and speckled with brown sugar!

"Stop, pot, stop!" said Maisie, and they both ate porridge until they were fit to burst. "Shall we make some for the people next door?" asked Maisie.

"No!" Her mother slipped the little iron pot under the table. "No, this is *our* secret. We won't tell *anyone*."

The next day, after the pot had given them both a delicious breakfast, Maisie went out to play with her friends at the other end of the village.

"Don't, pot, don't!" she begged, but the flow of porridge washed her chair out of the door. Soon the whole house was full of porridge. It came bubbling out of the chimney and slopping through the windows.

"Please, pot, please!" cried Maisie's mother clutching the branch of a tree to keep from being swept away by the rising tide of porridge. "Oh, pot, oooh!"

All through the village, people rushed out of their houses. "What's happening?" "A porridge flood!" "Quick, run for the hills!"

The noise and commotion reached the other end of the village, and Maisie ran outside. Howling villagers were clinging to the church spire and perching in the tree-tops. In the distance she could hear her mother's voice shouting: "Help, pot, *help!* No, pot, *nooooh!*"

Maisie guessed at once what had happened. She waded and swam as far as she could towards her house. Then, cupping her hands round her mouth, she called, "Stop, pot, stop!"

The little pot heard her. The bubbling stopped. And the village fell silent under a sea of cooling porridge.

But the magic porridge tasted delicious, even cold. The villagers ate their way from the top to the bottom of it. It took them all winter!

In spring, the witch returned for her little iron pot. "Did you take good care of it?" she asked Maisie, her crinkled eyes twinkling.

"No, I didn't," said Maisie, and her eyes twinkled too. "But *it* certainly took good care of *us!*"

THE FRIENDLY BEAR

When Otto the hunter caught the white bear, it was so big, so beautiful and so friendly that he decided to give it to the King of Denmark for Christmas. But as they travelled down the mountain together, night fell. "Let's get out of the cold," Otto said to him. "Look, there's a cottage!"

He knocked at the door and a voice inside said, "Why are you knocking? You've never bothered before." Anxious children's faces peered out of the window. "Oh, I'm sorry," said the farmer, opening the door. "I thought you were those terrible trolls."

"Trolls?" said Otto. "My friend the bear and I were just looking for somewhere safe to shelter until morning."

"You'll be better off in the caves, friend," said the farmer's wife. "That's where we're all going now. It's Christmas Eve, you know. And every Christmas Eve a pack of nasty trolls come down from the mountains and make themselves at home in our little house. They eat every scrap of food and drink all our beer. They break the furniture and smash the plates. Then, they all pile into our bed to sleep — and they don't even take their boots off!"

"It's just as well we came along when we did," said Otto. "Let *us* stay the night here, and I don't think you or your family will need to go to the caves this Christmas."

So the hunter bedded down in front of the kitchen fire, his bear curled up under the table, and the farmer and his wife went upstairs to their own bed.

At the stroke of midnight, shrieks of laughter and hideous howls rang out all around the cottage.

"RROOOOAAAOOOOAARR!!!" The white bear pounced out from under the table, grabbed the troll and threw him straight out the door and into the snow.

You never saw anything like the look on those troll's faces when they saw how big the "pussy cat" really was! They jumped through the window, climbed up the walls and fled up the chimney. The

Then the trolls shouted, *"Farmer Neils! We've come for our Christmas dinner, do you hear? What have you got for us this year? It had better be good — or else!"*

They forced the window open and tumbled in — the ugliest pack of creatures Otto had ever seen.

They opened every cupboard and drawer and began wolfing down all the food they could lay paws on — whole eggs, raw meat, cakes in their tins and all the sweets on the Christmas tree. Then they drank beer until they were reeling and rolling and singing at the tops of their voices.

"Oh, look," said a drunken troll. "Here's a sweet little pussy cat."

The bear opened one eye. "Have a sausage, little pussy," mumbled another troll, and he pushed a hot sausage up the bear's nose.

bear chased them out of the cottage and across the snow — back to the mountains.

Silence settled over the cottage. Farmer Neils and his wife crept downstairs. "I don't think you'll have any more trouble from those trolls," laughed Otto.

The grateful Mrs Neils gave him lots of the food that had been saved from the trolls, and he set off early the next day with his present for the King. By then, the news had reached every troll in the land: *"Don't go to Farmer Neils for your Christmas dinner! He's got himself the biggest pussy cat you've ever seen!"*

The ENCHANTED HORSE

On the 50th birthday of King Sabur of Persia, presents arrived at his palace from all over the land.

There were swords and silk and silver, coats and camels and caravans of cambrick cloth. But the best present of all was brought by a weird, ugly dwarf dressed all in black. He gave the king a horse carved in ebony, with a saddle of scarlet leather and a jingling golden harness.

"It's beautifully made," said King Sabur. "It looks *exactly* like a real horse."

"But it does not *move* like a real horse, your majesty," said the dwarf with an evil grin. "This is a magic horse. It can fly over the rainbow and to the far side of the farthest ocean."

King Sabur was overjoyed. And his only son, the handsome Prince Kamar, leapt into the saddle. "Tell me how it works!" he yelled. "Oh, do let me ride it!" But the king held up his hand for silence.

"This is such a wonderful present," he said to the ugly dwarf. "I must give you something in return. Ask anything you like, anything at all. If it's within my power, I will grant it."

"I thought you might say that,"

sneered the dwarf. "I ask for your only daughter, your *beautiful* daughter, as a bride." The king's face dropped.

"It is within your power to give her to me, I suppose?"

"Well, yes . . ." said the king unhappily.

"And you did promise me anything — anything at all?"

"Well, er, yes..." mumbled the king, and tears crept into his eyes.

"Don't do it, father!" shouted Prince Kamar from the horse's back. "Don't give away your only daughter, my *beautiful* sister, to this stranger. He tricked you into giving that promise. You don't have to keep it!"

"Ah, that's true," said the king. "I'm sorry, but I really don't think I can give you my only daughter, my *beautiful* daughter, for a bride."

The dwarf was furious, especially with Prince Kamar. He reached out

and pulled the reins of the horse.

Instantly, the strange beast sprang into life. Its hooves clattered on the marble floor. Then it bounded over the balcony rail and flew into the air, galloping upwards, higher and higher, while Kamar hung on for dear life.

The king gaped up at the flying horse. "Come back, Kamar! Come back down!"

"He can't!" sniggered the dwarf. "He doesn't know where the switch is that makes the horse come down. He will fly on up and up until he burns in the heat of the sun. You wouldn't give me your only daughter, so I took your only son. And now you will never see him again!"

King Sabur threw the dwarf into the darkest dungeon in his palace, and he cancelled his birthday party. In all his 50 years, he had never been so unhappy.

On the back of the flying horse, Kamar grew hotter and hotter as they climbed nearer and nearer to the sun.

He had tried everything to make the horse go down. He had shouted at it and kicked its flanks. He had pulled on its reins and heaved on its silken mane. Now he had given up hope.

"I'm sorry I shouted at you and kicked you and pulled on your mane," he said to the horse as if it were a real animal. And he patted its ebony neck.

And there it was, no bigger than a pin. Under the silken mane, Kamar felt the switch. He pushed it down.

The ebony horse plunged down out of the sky, and Kamar had to pull hard on the reins to keep it from diving into the sea.

Soon he came to the dry land of a foreign country. He flew over a magnificent city, and set the horse down on the roof of a glorious palace.

Climbing down through a skylight, he found himself in a beautiful bedroom. And on the bed lay a lady, fast asleep. Kamar instantly fell in love with her.

"Wake up, my lady," he whispered. "Who is your father? I must ask his permission to marry you." The Princess Shaleem woke up and saw Kamar's blue eyes and curling, jet-black hair. And she instantly fell in love with him.

"What are you doing in my daughter's bedroom, you thief, you burglar, you, you *foreigner*?"

The king was standing in the doorway, shaking his fist.

"I'm not a burglar, sire. I'm Prince Kamar of Persia. Please may I marry your daughter?"

"Certainly not!" shouted the king. "I shall have you beheaded for such impudence!"

The Princess Shaleem gave a little scream.

"That would not be honourable for a Prince of Persia," said Kamar politely. "I would fight your whole army for the right to marry the Princess."

"Then you shall!" laughed the king. He had an army of a thousand horsemen, so Kamar would be killed anyway. "You will need a war-horse?"

"Thank you, sire, but I have my own," said Kamar.

The next morning, at one end of the field behind the palace, a thousand horsemen stood ready.

The horsemen drew their swords, and a thousand sharp blades flashed in the sun. The war-horses' hooves tore up the grass as they quickened to a gallop.

Shaleem watched as Prince Kamar waited, perfectly calm. His black horse stood completely still, almost as if it was made of wood.

"Oh ride away, Kamar!" she called. "Don't be killed for my sake!" But Kamar waved to her, smiling, and picked up his horse's reins.

Just as the first horseman reached the prince, gnashing his teeth and waving his sword, Kamar pulled on the reins and rose up into the air. He flew *over* the thousand heads and the flashing swords, and landed on the other side.

The astonished horsemen turned back, barging into each other and falling over. But as they galloped back down the field, Kamar took off again and flew low over their heads, cutting the plumes off their helmets with his curved Persian sword.

An hour later, a thousand soldiers lay about on the grass, exhausted. They had *all* fallen off their horses. And they had *all* lost the plumes off their helmets.

Prince Kamar flew to the window where Princess Shaleem sat laughing and clapping her hands. Then he lifted her on to his saddle and flew across the blue sky.

King Sabur and his only daughter,

his *beautiful* daughter, were standing on the balcony of the Persian royal palace. At first they thought that the dark shape in the sky was a bird. Then they saw the black silk tail and the blonde hair stream out behind. And two riders were waving. In all his 50 years, King Sabur had never been so happy.

THE CREATION OF MAN

*O*ne dark and starry night a group of Red Indians sat huddled round a fire. Suddenly the oldest warrior stood up. His face was as old and as brown as the earth, and round his shoulders he wore a brightly-coloured blanket. He began to tell the story about the beginning of the world . . .

When Coyote, the desert dog, finished making the world, he took the wind, which was shaped like a sea-shell, and turned it upside down to form the sky. He put bright colours at the five corners of the world and a rainbow sprang up overhead and divided the night from the day. Then he sat back on his haunches and howled — and the sun and moon began to move across the sky.

Coyote planted the plains with trees and ponds and mountains and rivers, and he made all the animals.

"Last and best of all, I shall make *Man*," Coyote thought aloud. But the animals heard him and wanted to help. So they all sat down in a circle in the forest: Coyote, Grizzly Bear, Lion, Honey Bear, Deer, Sheep, Beaver, Owl and Mouse.

"You can make Man whatever shape you like," said Lion, "but I think he should have sharp teeth for tearing meat, and long claws, too."

"Like yours?" asked Coyote.

"Well, yes. Like mine," said Lion. "He will need fur, of course. And a big, loud, roaring voice."

"Like yours?" asked Coyote.

"Like mine," said Lion. "Nobody wants a voice like yours," Grizzly interrupted. "You frighten everyone away. Man must be able to walk on his back legs and creep up on things and hug them in his arms until they're squashed flat."

"Like you do?" asked Coyote. "Well, yes. Like I do," replied Grizzly.

Deer, who trembled nervously and kept glancing over her shoulder, said: "What's all this about tearing meat and squashing things? It isn't nice. Man has to be able to know when he's in danger and run away quickly. He should have ears like sea-shells to hear every tiny sound. And eyes like the Moon, which sees everything. Oh, and antlers, of course. He will need antlers."

"Like yours?" asked Coyote.

"Well, yes. Like mine," said Deer.

"Like *yours?*" scoffed Sheep. "What good are antlers? Long, spiky things that get caught in every branch and bush! How is Man going to be able to *butt* things? Now if he had horns on either side of his head . . ."

"Like yours?" asked Coyote.

Sheep only sniffed. He did not like being interrupted.

Then Beaver stood up and said: "You are forgetting the most important thing of all — Man's *tail.* Long thin tails are all right for

swatting flies, I suppose. But Man must have a broad, flat tail. How else can he build dams in the river?"

"Like yours?" asked Coyote.

"Nobody builds dams like *mine*," said the Beaver, in a very boastful way.

"Man sounds far too *big*," squeaked Mouse. "He would be better being small."

"You're all out of your wits-wits-woo!" hooted Owl. "What about wings? If you want Man to be the best animal of all, he must be able to fly. He *must have wings!*"

"Like yours?" asked Coyote.

"Is that all you can say?" Owl complained. "Don't *you* have any ideas?"

Coyote jumped to his feet and prowled to the centre of the circle. "You silly animals! I don't know what I was thinking about when I made you! You all want Man to look exactly like you!"

"And I suppose Man should be just like *you*, Coyote," growled Honey Bear.

"Then how could anyone tell us apart?" replied Coyote. "Everyone would point at

me and say, 'There goes Man'. And they would point at Man and say, 'There goes Coyote'. No, no. Man must be *different*."

"But with a tail!" shouted Beaver. "And wings!" hooted Owl. "And antlers!" bayed Deer. "And horns!" baaed Sheep. "And a roar!" roared Grizzly. "And be very small," squeaked Mouse. But nobody heard him. They were too busy fighting.

Biting and butting and clawing and chewing, the animals fought each other across the forest floor while Coyote stood by and shook his head. Fur and feathers and hooves and horns flew all over the place.

47

Coyote picked them up, and putting them together again he made all sorts of new, peculiar animals — like the camel and the giraffe.

Soon all the animals lay in an exhausted heap, too tired to fight any more. "I think I may have the answer," said Coyote at last.

The animals blinked at him, and some of them snarled. But Coyote spoke to them all the same.

"Bear was right to say that Man should walk on his back legs. That means he can reach into the trees. And Deer was right to say that Man should have sharp ears and good eyes. But if Man had wings he would bump his head on the sky. The only part of a bird that he needs is Eagle's long claws. I think I'll call them fingers.

"And Lion was right when he said that Man should have a big voice. But he needs a little voice, too, so that he's not too frightening. I think Man should be smooth like Fish, who has no fur to make him hot and itchy. But most important of all," said Coyote finally, "Man must be more clever and cunning than *any* of you!"

"Like you are," muttered all the animals.

"Well, yes, thank you." said Coyote. "Like I am." There was a lot of angry growling and hissing and the animals began to shout: "Sit down Coyote! Nobody likes your silly ideas!"

"Well," said Coyote patiently. "Let's have a competition. We'll each make a model of Man out of mud. Tomorrow we can look at all the models and decide which is the best."

So all the animals rushed away to fetch water and make mud. Owl made a model with wings. Deer made a model with large ears and wide eyes. Beaver made a model with a broad, flat tail. Mouse made a very small model. But Coyote made Man.

The sun went down before any of them could finish their models. So they went to sleep on the forest floor. All except Coyote.

He fetched water from the river and poured it over all the other models. Beaver's mud tail was washed away. Deer's mud antlers were washed away. Owl's mud wings were washed away.

Coyote blew into the nose of his model of Man made of mud. And when the other animals woke up, they found that there was a new animal in the forest. His name was Man.'

With these words
the old warrior sat
down, wrapping his
blanket round him.
As the glow from
the fire died down,
he sat as silent as the
earth staring into the darkness.
And in the distance the cry of the
coyote floated across the plains.

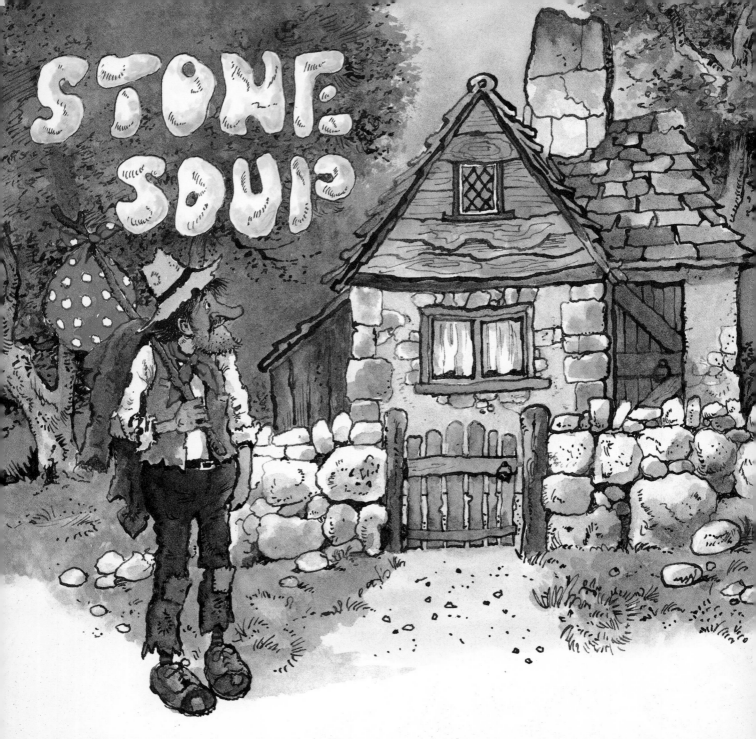

STONE SOUP

The poor tramp was very, very hungry. "I've been walking through these woods for days and I haven't eaten a thing," he said to himself as he came to a little cottage in the clearing. "Whoever lives here is bound to give me something to eat."

But the tramp had chosen the worst possible place to ask for food. This was the cottage of Miss Parsimony — the meanest woman in the whole forest. Her larder was always full, but her dishes were always empty. She never invited people home to tea, and she never ate any of the good things that grew in her garden. "You have to *save*," she used to say. "You never know when friends are going to call." But to tell the truth, Miss Parsimony was so mean, that she had no friends at all.

Knock, knock, knock. The tramp rapped on the kitchen door.

"Who are you? What do you want?" shouted Miss Parsimony. "Something for nothing, I suppose. Everybody wants something for nothing these days!"

Behind her shoulder, the tramp could see strings of onions hanging on the kitchen wall, and on the shelves row upon row of tins, bottles and jars. His mouth watered. "Go away!" the old woman shouted. "You'll get nothing from me! I've nothing to spare!"

The tramp could not help noticing how very thin and pale the face was watching him through the crack in the door. Miss Parsimony looked in need of a good meal, too. "Time for the Stone Soup Trick," he said to himself.

"I was only going to, um, ask for some water, dear lady," he said smiling. "I was about to cook myself a pot of delicious stone soup."

The crack in the door widened. "Did you say, *stone* soup?"

"Yes," said the tramp. "I've got the magic stone. I only need some water."

"Wait there!" she snapped. And a moment later she came back with a pot of water.

"How kind," said the tramp. "Won't you join me? I don't want to boast, but they do say my stone soup's the best in the world."

"Never heard of it!" said the woman, as he unpacked an old tin and began to make a small fire outside the garden gate.

Miss Parsimony went indoors again, but she watched him from behind the curtains. The tramp picked up a big stone and put it into the pan of water. Then he sat back and watched it boil. Suddenly, the kitchen door opened and Miss Parsimony came and peered over the wall.

"Are you going to eat *that*?" she said, making a face.

"You're quite right," said the tramp. "Stone soup is always better with an onion. But I'll just have to make do."

A moment later, a hand came over the wall holding a small onion. "Here," said Miss Parsimony sourly.

"Thank you madam," he said, adding the onion, then tasting the soup. "Mmm it's delicious." Miss Parsimony watched with wider and wider eyes.

"I can see what you're thinking. Real stone soup is always better with onions *and* a tin of beans. But I'll just have to make do with the onions and the water."

"I might just have some beans," said Miss Parsimony. And she fetched a tin from the kitchen shelf.

"I can't possibly accept this," said the tramp emptying the beans into the water, "unless you agree to share the soup with me."

Miss Parsimony scowled down at the bubbling soup and wrinkled up her nose.

"Ah, I know what you're thinking," said the tramp. "You ladies always like lots of mushrooms as well as onions and beans in your stone soup. But, I suppose we'll just have to make do."

"I've got some mushrooms!" exclaimed Miss Parsimony. And she rushed round to the back of the house to pick some. And into the pot they went.

"Oh of course, it's a, a funny colour," apologised the tramp. "It's er, it's the beef that gives stone soup its wonderful colour, as well as the onion, beans and mushrooms."

"Beef! Beef!" exclaimed Miss Parsimony, by now quite carried away with the thought of eating real stone soup. So she fetched a tin of beef stew from the cupboard and added it to the soup. The tramp tasted it again.

"A turnip or a potato would make this fit for a king to eat!"

"Both! Both!" cried Miss Parsimony, and she dug furiously in the vegetable patch for a sweet white potato *and* a purply turnip.

"Does it need any salt?"

The thick soup heaved and plopped in the pan — onions and beans and mushrooms and beef and turnip and potato and salt — not to mention the tramp's stone. The smell was mouth-watering. Together they carried the pan into the cottage and Miss Parsimony laid the table for two.

He suggested cheese to go with the

soup. *She* suggested wine. *He* thought a crusty roll would be nice. *She* fetched out an apple pie for pudding.

"Oh, that was the best meal I've eaten in my life!" said Miss Parsimony afterwards. "That stone of yours is really wonderful."

"It's yours, dear lady, take it," said the tramp.

"What? Are you really giving the magic stone to me?" she said, her eyes brimming with tears. "Nobody has ever given me such a wonderful present. Just think! I can invite people round to tea and cook them stone soup like this every single day. And it won't cost me a penny!"

"Of course, of course," said the tramp pulling on his coat. "But do remember to add a little salt for flavouring."

"No, I won't forget!"

"And onion and beans and mushrooms and some beef."

"No, I mustn't forget them."

"And a potato and a turnip, of course."

"I'll follow your recipe exactly."

"I do find people like their stone soup best with a few little extras," said the tramp, waving goodbye from the gate.

The Forest Troll

Once upon a time there was an old woman who lived with her three sons in a little wooden house on the edge of a dark forest.

One year when winter was coming the old woman asked her eldest son to go into the forest and chop down a tree for firewood.

"Do I *have* to?" the oldest boy asked. "When it gets really cold we could all go to bed. Then we wouldn't need to build a fire."

"Don't be so lazy!" the old woman said. "We can't stay in bed all winter. You're the strongest of my sons, so go and fetch some wood."

The oldest boy didn't like hard work, but he finally set off for the forest, carrying the smallest axe he could find. When he got there he went to the most rotten tree he could see.

"This shouldn't be too hard," and he lifted up the axe to start chopping. He had just tapped the tree once when he felt a thump on his shoulder. He turned around and behind him he saw the ugliest, most revolting troll you could ever imagine. The creature had one red eye in the centre of his forehead and his purple nose was knobbly and twisted like the root of an old tree.

"Hey, you, superman!" shouted the troll. "If you chop down one tree in my forest I'll break you into fifty pieces."

The boy threw down his axe. He ran home as fast as his legs could carry him and he told his family all about the giant.

"Fancy being afraid of a stupid old troll!" sneered the second son. "*I* wouldn't be afraid."

The next morning the second son picked up a bigger axe and set off to fetch some wood. As soon as he got to the forest he found a large tree that looked like it would make enough wood to last the whole winter.

Thwack! Thwack . . ack!
The sound of his axe echoed through the forest.

But before he'd got halfway through the tree the troll appeared.

"Hey, you, muscles! What do you think you're doing? You lift that axe once more and I'll break you into a hundred pieces."

"Don't think I'm s-scared of an old t-t-troll like you." "You c-can't f-frighten *me*. I'm going to chop down this t-tree."

"We'll see about that!" And he lifted a long arm up into the tree and pulled off a big branch. He snapped it across his knee and started breaking it into tiny twigs.

The second brother saw how strong the troll was and ran off home as fast as he could. He was shaking with fear when he arrived home and his elder brother greeted him.

"Well, where's all the wood then?"

"I met the nasty troll. He chased me out of the forest. He was much too strong to argue with. Why, he was fifty feet . . ."

Just then the old woman's youngest son butted in. "*I* wouldn't be scared of him. I'm sure I wouldn't. I'll go and fetch the wood."

"What, *you*? You're *much* too young to chop down a tree with that troll you wouldn't stand a chance."

"Oh please, please let me go."

In the end, despite her fears, the old woman said her youngest son should be allowed to try his luck in the forest.

So the next day the third son picked up the biggest axe in the house. It was so heavy he could hardly carry it. He went to the kitchen cupboard and took out a firm white ball of cheese. When the brothers saw him putting the cheese into his bag they laughed.

"What do you want that for? Are you going to have a picnic with your friend the troll?" But the young boy did not answer, and he went off to the forest, dragging the huge axe behind him.

When he reached the forest he went to the biggest tree he could find. It was about twenty feet thick and so tall he could not see the top. He struggled to lift the huge axe, but he had to let it drop . . . and yet again the sound brought the troll pounding through the forest.

"Oh no! Not *another* one! And no more than a boy! If you chop that tree I'll break you into a *thousand* pieces."

The boy looked straight at the ugly troll. "You just try it and I'll crush *you* like

I'll crush this stone." As he spoke the boy took the big white cheese and squeezed it hard between his hands. The cheese squirted everywhere — and the biggest blob hit the troll in his great red eye.

"All right! All right!" shouted the troll. "That's enough. Don't crush me like that stone. You can chop down any trees you want — no, I'll chop them for you if you like. I'll, I'll cut them into logs and take them back to your house."

From that day on the troll made sure that the old woman and her family had all the firewood they needed.

WISER Than The CZAR

Every day, on its way from the palace to the cathedral, the Czar's coach passed a poor tumbledown farmhouse. But on one particular day, the Czar saw the farmer leaning on the fence smoking a pipe and he stopped the coach to speak to him.

The farmer fell to his knees. "Your most gracious royal highness. You do the greatest honour to me, to my farm, to the smallest pebble in the last clod of earth in stopping your coach here and setting foot on my humble land."

The Czar was taken aback. "You don't talk much like a peasant. Who taught you such good manners?"

"My daughter says that words are the most priceless things we own, and that I must use them well."

"A wise girl, your daughter."

"Oh sire!" cried the farmer. "She's the wisest person in all Russia. I don't know where she gets it from. I've got no brains myself to speak of."

"The wisest person in all Russia, you say?" said the Czar, twirling his long moustache.

"Yes, sire!"

"*Wiser than me?*"

"Oh." The farmer gulped. "What have I said?" But the Czar had leaped back into his coach and was driven away at great speed.

Later that day the Czar was back again. "Here! Peasant!" he shouted, leaning out of the coach with a basket of eggs in his hands. "Your wise daughter can do something for me. But heaven help her if she does it badly. Give her these three dozen eggs and tell her to hatch them by tomorrow morning." And he clattered away amid a cloud of dust.

The farmer stared down at the basket of eggs. They were bright red. "What kind of eggs *are* they?" he asked his daughter when he had taken them indoors.

"Your father said you were wise," called the Czar. "But you must be an idiot to plant *boiled* beans. What kind of harvest do you expect from them?"

"Exactly the same as the good Czar expected when he asked me to hatch hard-boiled eggs, Sir. Good morning."

The Czar blushed and hurried off, knowing that the peasant girl had beaten him at his own game.

She took one in her hand and felt its weight. "They're hard-boiled eggs, father, that's what they are. I can't hatch these."

"Oh! I knew the Czar would punish us. He's just looking for an excuse to banish us."

But his daughter said, "I'll think of something, Papa. Don't worry."

The next morning the Czar's coach stopped beside the farm fence. The Czar looked out in amazement — the farmer's daughter was walking behind the plough planting beans in the ground. She chanted as she went,

"*Boiled beans I sew*
But will boiled beans grow?"

The next day the farmer opened the cottage door and found a reel of cotton on the doorstep. Alongside it lay the Czar's gilt-edged visiting card. The message on it read:

Tell your WISE daughter to make me two sails for my sailing ship out of this cotton by tomorrow — or I shall banish you both to Siberia.

The old farmer tore his hair. "Oh whatever shall we *do*, daughter?"

His daughter put the reel of cotton in her apron pocket. "Don't fret, father,"

she said, writing a note on the back of the visiting card. "Take this message to the palace."

She broke a twig off the apple tree and put it with the card. The note read:

I am sure you know how poor my father is. I am afraid he cannot afford to buy me a spinning-wheel and a loom. But if the good Czar will make me a spinning-wheel and a loom out of this twig, I will be most happy to make sails for his sailing ship out of a single reel of cotton.

When the Czar got her message, he laughed out loud. "By heaven, she's a clever girl!" And he called his messenger. "Take this wine glass to the miserable little farm on the north road. Tell the girl who lives there that if she can empty the sea with this wine glass by morning, I'll marry her!"

When the girl heard the message, she laughed out loud. She picked up the little stool from under the kitchen table, and, borrowing the messenger's horse she rode all the way to the palace.

Curtseying deeply to the Czar, she set down the stool.

"Most dear Czar," she said. "All Russia loves you and I love you more than all Russia. Nothing would please me more than to do as you ask. But I have one slight problem in emptying the sea overnight."

"Aha!" said the Czar. "Not so clever after all, eh?"

"No, no, not clever at all. Of course I can empty the sea itself. But as soon as I finish, the rivers will start to fill it up again. So if you would just dam up all the rivers in the world with this stool, I'll willingly empty the sea for you with this wine glass."

The Czar laughed delightedly. "By heaven, your father was quite right. You *are* wiser than me. But I'm wise enough to know a good wife when I see one — and to prove it I'll marry you this very day!"

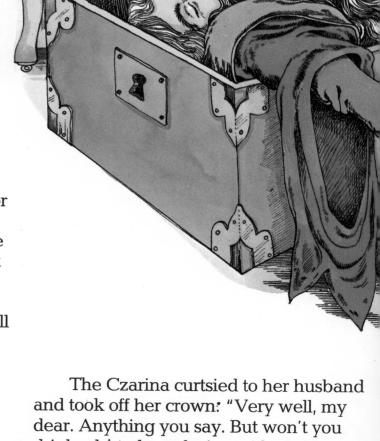

The girl put her head on one side, thoughtfully. "I might marry you, your royal highness, if you will make me one promise."

"What! You impudent young th . . . Well, what do you want?"

"Promise me that if you ever get tired of me and send me away, you'll let me take with me the one thing I want most from the whole palace."

"Oh, is that all? Run and get ready. I'll be waiting for you at the church."

So the poor farmer's daughter became the Czarina of all Russia. And the couple lived very happily together for many years.

But as he got older the Czar became awkward and restless and began to pick quarrels with everyone in the palace — even the Czarina. "You think you're so clever!" he stormed at her one day. "Well go back where you came from and take your wisdom with you! I'm sick of you. Get out!"

The Czarina curtsied to her husband and took off her crown: "Very well, my dear. Anything you say. But won't you drink a last glass of wine with me?"

When the glasses were brought, she slipped a sleeping potion into the Czar's wine. A minute later, he was sprawled across his throne, snoring.

The Czarina called for a large trunk and put the Czar into it and locked it fast. Then she called the palace servants, and had them load the trunk on to a cart. She took off her fine gown and put back on her patched, farming clothes. Then she

drove the cart back to the farm on the north road.

When the Czar woke up, he was lying on a straw mattress on the floor of the miserable shack. "What am I doing here? How dare you kidnap the crowned head of all Russia. I'll have your head for this, you insolent woman!"

"But my dear husband," said his wife, looking up from her sewing. "You made me a promise on our wedding day that if you were ever to send me away, I could take with me the one thing I wanted most from the whole palace. And I wanted you."

And only then did the Czar realise just how lucky he was to have found such a wise and wonderful wife.

THE DANCING FAIRIES

Once upon a time, on the Swedish island of Göv, there lived a servant called Little Anders. He worked as a groom in the stables of Mr Strale, the clergyman. Now Little Anders was a dreamer. He dreamed all day and all night about elves and fairies, and he often fell asleep when he was supposed to be working. And, one hot Midsummer's Day, he slept right through the afternoon.

"Wake up, Little Anders," said his master. "It's late! Hurry down to the meadow and fetch my horse. We must lock him up safely before dark or the fairies will whisk him away."

The full Midsummer moon was shining brightly by the time Little Anders reached the meadow. Suddenly he heard the strangest music from far above his head. Then, as he listened, a cloud of winged fairies sailed down a moonbeam and landed in the middle of a circle of dark grass, where they danced to the music of a fairy orchestra. Leading them was their Queen, who was taller than the others and very beautiful. She wore a silver crown and her dress sparkled with precious stones.

Little Anders crept closer and closer to watch. Then the Queen called out: "Stop! There's a stranger present!" The music ceased, and the dancers stood like statues. "You'd better go home," said the Queen, turning to Little Anders. "Or you may find yourself bewitched."

"I'd rather dance with you," he replied, and no sooner had he spoken than he found himself in the middle of the fairy ring, with the Queen in his arms.

They danced for hours, but then the Queen cried out: "Stop! It's almost cock-crow. It's time we were back in Fairyland!" And the fairies flew off, leaving poor Anders dancing by himself.

His master found him there in the morning, still dancing. He danced all the way home, and he danced up and down the stairs. He danced all day and he danced all night. Indeed, he danced for three whole days!

Then, nearly a month later, on the night of the full moon, Little Anders climbed out of his window just before midnight and ran all the way to the meadow. Once again he heard the wonderful music and saw the fairy dancers sailing through the sky, led by their Queen. This time she seemed more beautiful than ever.

Folding their wings, they all began dancing with Anders and the Queen in the centre of the fairy ring. And, as before, they danced happily until dawn. Then the Queen said: "Stop! It's almost cock-crow and we must be off. Goodbye, Little Anders. Hurry home."

"No!" shouted Anders. "This time I'm going with you!" And, clutching the Queen's robe, he sailed with her up a moonbeam and into the sky, the other fairies following behind.

But this was not the last of Little Anders. Old Mr Strale told everyone that on Midsummer Nights, when the moon was full, he would see Anders dancing in the meadow. From midnight until cock-crow, circled round by all the winged creatures of Fairyland, he danced in the arms of the beautiful fairy Queen.

NARANA'S STRANGE JOURNEY

It was a bitterly cold but sunny day when Narana set off on her long walk back to her village. She had been staying with her sister in the hills, and now she was returning to her husband and children on the coast.

With her snow-shoes, shaped like tennis rackets, Narana was able to walk easily across the soft snow. But suddenly the weather changed. The wind grew stronger and stronger, whipping up the snow, and poor Narana could hardly see where she was going. Soon a blizzard was raging, and the wind was so fierce that it knocked her off her feet. Over and over she rolled, blown by the storm, until she found herself wedged between what seemed to be two great trees.

At last the gale died down and the skies began to clear. But Narana had no idea where she was. The hills ahead lay in four curved ridges—like the fingers of a huge hand. Everywhere there were spiky brown bushes. As night fell she reached the top of the highest ridge and found a hollow where she could shelter from the wind. Tired and miserable, she curled up and went to sleep.

In the morning Narana walked along the ridge. On one side the slopes fell away, covered in strange bushes. On the other, the hillside was marked with enormous blue streaks, like underground rivers.

She slithered down between them and began climbing the other side. She walked for hours, every now and then hearing gurgling, bubbling noises under her feet.

"What a strange place this is," she thought. "I've never been anywhere like it before. I wonder where I am."

Then she came to a great flat plateau, and in the distance she could see a vast black forest that seemed to touch the sky. Narana trudged towards it, but before she could get there darkness came again and she found a large wood where she could shelter for the night.

Narana woke tired and very hungry. She ate a handful of snow to quench her

you and what are you *doing* here, where nobody ever comes?"

At first Narana could not speak. She looked all around but could see no-one. "I—I am Narana," she said at last to the skies, her voice trembling with fear. "I was on my journey home when I lost my way in the storm. Who are you . . . *what* are you? A mountain ghost?"

"*No, I am a giant!*" rumbled the voice as the earth shook again. "*My name is Kinak. I sleep here all alone*

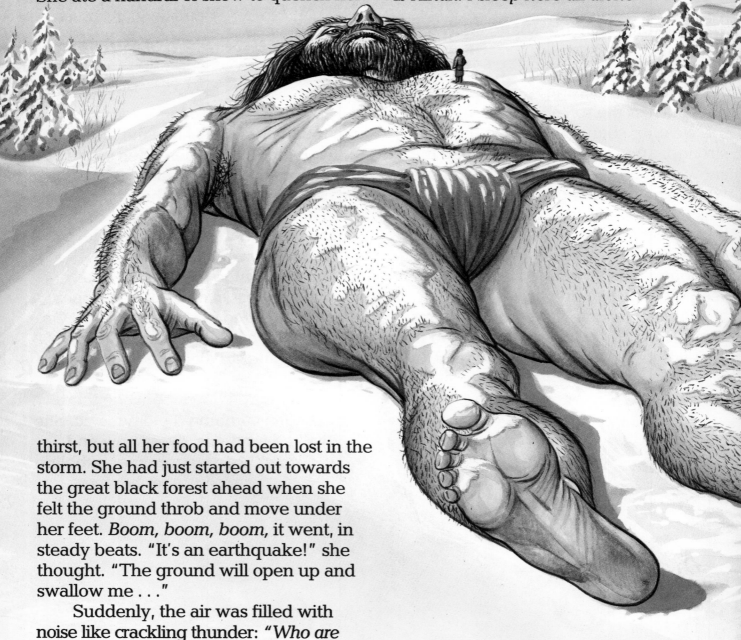

thirst, but all her food had been lost in the storm. She had just started out towards the great black forest ahead when she felt the ground throb and move under her feet. *Boom, boom, boom,* it went, in steady beats. "It's an earthquake!" she thought. "The ground will open up and swallow me . . ."

Suddenly, the air was filled with noise like crackling thunder: "*Who are*

on the great plain so that I can stretch without crushing the villages or the trees."

"But where *are* you?" asked Narana, still looking around.

"*I'm underneath you, Narana. You have been climbing over me for two days. You started on my left hand and now you are over my heart. I expect you can feel it.*"

"Yes. Yes I can. Oh, I do hope I haven't hurt you."

The earth shook again, even more violently than before, and Narana was thrown over and over . . . as the giant's laughter rang out for miles across the plains.

"*No, little one, you didn't hurt me. Not even a tickle. Herds of reindeer can be a nuisance, but one human is nothing.*"

The giant let out a chuckle, and Narana was once again dumped in the snow. "*I first saw you when you were curled up asleep between my thumb and finger. Then you clambered down my hand, over my wrist, up my arm and on to my stomach. That's my beard ahead of you. But I can't see you very well now without lifting my head and looking down my nose. Can you climb up on to my face?*"

It took Narana a long time to scale the heights to Kinak's face. With his forest of a beard she found the best way was to go along the side of his neck and climb up his ear.

"*You had better go right along to the end of my nose. I don't want to swallow you by mistake.*"

Narana asked the giant if he could whisper because she found his voice frightening.

And when he spoke, she fell over. But she still had to yell, even from his nose. "I'll have to go soon, Kinak," she said. "I'm two days late and my family will be worried to death about me."

"Well, if you have to. But I shall miss you Narana. It's very lonely out here some times. Oh well, at least I'll be able to have a good stretch and roll over. I've not moved since I first noticed you for fear of crushing you."

"Thank you, Kinak, that's very kind," said Narana. "But where am I?"

"It doesn't really matter. Where do you live?"

"The village of Tivnu, by the sea."

"Oh, not far then. I can blow you there."

"What do you mean?" asked Narana.

"Climb on to my bottom lip and sit with your back to me."

Narana did as the giant said and sat on his lip, waiting. Far below her the earth began to rise up as Kinak breathed

in deeply. He puffed gently and she flew off his lip and shot through the air, twisting and rolling and turning like a whirlwind. A few seconds later she landed in a deep drift of snow, safe and sound. She stood up, brushed the loose snow off her — and there, just a short walk away, was the village of Tivnu.

As Narana began to walk joyously towards the houses, she thought she heard the faint sound of rumbling in the distance, like short rolls of thunder. It was almost like the sound of a giant, sobbing.

MASTER of the LAKE

In a small hut in a far-off land, there lived an old couple who were very poor. They had no sheep, nor horses, nor goats — not even a hive of bees to give them honey. When they died, they left their son Avram nothing but a few strands of flax scattered on the floor.

Avram took these down to the lake, dipped them into the water and set about plaiting the wet strands into a rope. While he was working, the fearsome Master of the Lake rose from its watery depths and stood before him. Though he was very frightened, Avram tried not to show it.

"What are you doing here?" the green, bearded giant cried.

"I'm plaiting a rope. When it's ready, I'm going to hang your lake from the clouds!"

This strange, brave reply struck fear into the Master. "No, no, boy!" he cried. "Don't touch my lake, I beg you! I'll grant you any wish you like, but leave my waters in peace."

Avram thought hard. What should he ask of the giant? The lake was famous locally for the beautiful wild horses that watered there so, he made up his mind. "Give me your finest horse, and I'll not touch your lake."

"Oh no! Those horses are my fame and my strength!" cried the Master. "I can't grant *that* wish."

"As you please," replied Avram. "Then I shall have to hang your lake."

The Master of the Lake was silent. Perhaps he suspected a trick. "Well, boy," he said at last, "if you are strong enough to hang my lake, you won't refuse a test of strength between us first. We'll race round the lake. If you overtake me, I'll grant your wish."

"Agreed!" said Avram. "There's just one thing. I have a younger brother. He's sleeping in the bushes over there. If you can beat him first, *then* I'll race you round the lake myself."

The giant went into the bushes at the edge of the lake — and out scampered a frightened hare. At once the Master of the Lake gave chase. But of course, he could not catch the hare, no matter how fast he ran.

"I'll beat you yet!" he shouted to Avram in a rage. "Let's fight!"

Avram agreed. "Oh, but first you must beat my old grandfather. If you can knock him off his feet, I'll leave the lake to you. There he is, resting in that hollow. He's er, a heavy sleeper, so you'll have to give him a crack over the head to wake him."

Off went the Master to the hollow where a big brown bear was dozing. He gave the bear a crack over the head with a big stick — which did not please the bear. Leaping up, it seized the Master of the Lake in its strong arms and threw him crashing to the ground.

Limping back to Avram, the giant cried, "How strong your grandfather is! I've no strength left to fight you. But give me one last chance.

I have a dapple-grey horse — the finest in my herd. Let's see which of us can carry her round the lake."

"You try first," said Avram. So, the Master lifted the horse on to his shoulders and staggered with her round the lake. With a triumphant shout, he set her down in front of Avram. "Now it's *your* turn!"

Avram put aside his rope and went up to the horse. "Hah! You lifted the mare on your shoulders. Now watch me carry her between my knees!" And he mounted, dug his heels into her flanks, and rode round the lake at a gallop.

The giant saw he was beaten. Patting the dapple-grey mare one last time, he gave her to Avram. And what a fine horse she was, with a thick forelock, powerful legs, sharp ears, and a broad, deep chest. Avram mounted this handsome mare and galloped home.

The Nightingale

There was once a nightingale who lived in a large crystal cage. She belonged to a rich Persian merchant who loved, more than anything else, to listen to her sweet song. If he sometimes detected a sad note, he quickly dismissed it from his thoughts.

"My nightingale has everything a bird could possibly want," he told himself. "I'm sure she's the happiest bird in Persia."

One day the merchant announced that he was going on a long journey to buy silks and perfumes from the East. On the way he would pass the nightingale's first home — a forest whose floor was carpeted with flowers. Was there anything the nightingale wished him to say to her brothers and sisters?

"Just tell them I'm well," she said, "and ask if they have a message for me."

The merchant did as she requested, and on returning from his journey, he immediately went to see her.

"I asked one of your brothers if he had a message for you," he said in a puzzled voice. "But all he did was to fall to the ground and lie completely still among the flowers. I picked him up, but he still didn't move, so I decided he must be dead. I gently put him down and was

just turning to leave when he fluttered his wings and flew high up into a tree. I called to him again and again to say something, but he ignored all my pleas. I think your brothers and sisters must have forgotten you."

The nightingale bowed her head in grief. All day long she refused to eat or drink any of the tasty morsels which were brought to her.

And when the merchant came to see her the next morning, he found her lying at the bottom of the cage. Not a feather moved as he begged her to fly to her perch and sing. Then he opened the cage, carefully picked her up and gently stroked her neck. But still she did not move. Stricken with grief, he thought she must have died. So, with tears in his eyes, he took her outside and laid her on the grass.

And as he walked back to his house, he turned to look at her one last time. And then he saw her brown wings quiver in the sunlight and her beak open in a cry of joy and happiness.

The nightingale soared into the sky. "Thank you for the message from my brother," she called. "It was the best message I've ever received."

And away she flew, to the forest whose floor was carpeted with flowers.

ANANSI AND THE PYTHON

Deep in the jungle, on the muddy banks of the River Niger, lay an enormous snake — a coiling, hungry python. He ate the jungle animals, he ate the village cows, and he ate anyone who strayed too close to the river.

The villagers were so terrified that they called out to the Sky god, "Save us from the monster, man-eating Python!"

"No," said the god of the Sky.

"I made Python. I won't unmake him. But if anyone can put a stop to his murderous ways, I'll reward them with a present."

The villagers threw up their hands and groaned. "Who's clever enough to destroy Python? Who's brave enough to try?"

Close to the village lived Anansi, the spider-man. When he heard the Sky god's words, he said, "I'll tackle Python.

Give me a bowl of wine, a basket of eggs and a long rope. Then cut down a tall tree, strip off the branches, and carry it to the river."

The villagers carried the tree down to the river, and ran home as fast as they could, fearing the snake would eat them up.

But Python just lay dozing in his hole. Anansi crept right up and sat down outside. "No, no," he said in a loud voice. "You're wrong. Python's really nice, so nice I've brought him a present of wine and eggs."

Then Anansi moved to the other side of the hole and said in a squeaky voice, "But Python's *evil!* He eats up cows and people and scares us half to death!"

Creeping back to the other side, Anansi said out loud, "Rubbish! I won't sit here and listen to you insulting my friend! Take that, you liar! Take that! And that!" And he jumped and thumped on the mud. "Ugh! Oh! Ow! Take *that!*"

Python roused himself and poked his head out of the hole. He saw no-one there but Anansi, panting and muttering to himself, "That's sent *him* packing. *He* won't insult dear Python again!"

Then seeing Python, Anansi leaped up, bowed, and presented him with the wine and the eggs. Python opened his huge, hinged jaws, and swallowed bowl, basket and all. "How kind," he hissed.

"O mighty snake!" cried Anansi, "I am so honoured to meet you."

Python gave a smirk. "You seem more intelligent than most people."

"Oh yes! People are *so* stupid," Anansi agreed. "*They* say you're only long enough to coil round a cow . . ."

"What?" hissed Python.

"Well, *I* tell them you're easily long enough to coil round a hut . . ."

"A what?"

". . . or even a whole village. Exactly how long are you, Mr Python?"

Python shuffled a short way out of his hole. He was monstrously big. But Anansi hid his fear and said, "I still can't judge. Come right out and let me measure you."

Python slid, coil after glistening coil, out of his hole. Anansi gulped, but said, "You see this tree? If you lie beside it, I can measure you."

The eggs and wine were making Python very sleepy, so he grinned foolishly and slithered over to the tree.

"Okay, if you like."

"Now," said Anansi, "if I tie a piece of rope round you every ten paces, I can count up the ropes and work out how many paces long you are . . ."

"Okay," said Python yawning. Anansi tied the first rope round his tail and round the tree. "Your knots are rather tight," grumbled Python, as Anansi went on tying rope after rope.

"Stop complaining," Anansi scolded "Stretch out as long as you can — don't you want to be known as the Longest Python in the World?"

So Python stretched and strained, and Anansi went on tying knots. Last of all he tied Python's neck to the tree, and stood back to admire his handiwork.

"Well? How big am I?" asked Python. "Hurry up and measure me!"

"I can see from here," sniggered Anansi. "Your body's awfully big, but your brain's very, very small. How will you eat your next villager, Mr Python? How will you swallow your next cow? I've put a stop to you and your murderous ways for ever!"

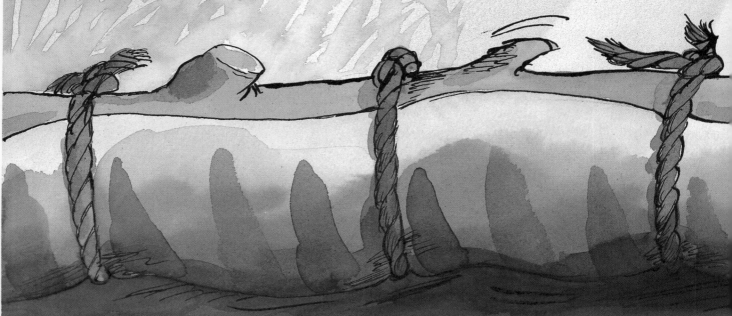

When Python saw Anansi dancing triumphantly up and down the tree trunk, he struggled and strained to get free. His tongue flickered wickedly. But he was tied so tight that he could not move a muscle.

"Did you see that?" called Anansi, grinning up at the sky. "Did you see how I put a stop to Python?"

"I saw, Anansi, and I remember what I promised," replied the Sky god. "Here is your reward." And the Sky god leaned down out of the heavens and gave Anansi a small box. "Inside is wisdom — enough for a lifetime. Your cleverness will make you famous, and your trickery will keep you safe."

So that is how Anansi, the spider-man, came to be the cleverest person in the whole jungle — even cleverer than he had been before.

And Python? Well, he just floated away on his tree trunk, down the River Niger, deeper and deeper into the deep, dark jungle.

Willow Pattern

Great was the power of the mandarins of old China, and great was their wealth. One such mandarin lived in a mansion two storeys high. While common men slept on the ground beneath humble roofs, the mandarin slept each night on a level with the blossom of his peach trees.

The gardens of his mansion were a paradise of pools and flowers, lawns, bridges and pavilions. But the greatest beauty in the gardens of the mandarin was the mandarin's daughter, Li-chi.

The mandarin often worked all day in his library, with his secretary — a young and handsome man named Chang. While the mandarin ate sumptuous meals, Chang would walk in the gardens. He liked to stand on a bridge which led to the island of a large ornamental lake, and watch the golden fish swim by below.

Li-chi, too, loved to stand on the bridge and watch the golden fish. She loved still more to watch the sloe-black eyes of Chang and to drink in his words, as he spoke of Pekin and Anyang and the distant lands of Tibet.

Before long, Li-chi loved Chang, and Chang loved Li-chi — although he said, "You are high above me, being the daughter of the mandarin. I am nothing but a humble secretary."

"But you own a garden of wisdom and the flowers of poetry," she said. "You are therefore as noble and rich as my father. Let us stand beneath the orange blossom and promise to love one another for ever!" So hand in hand they stood beneath the orange tree and vowed vows of love. But the mandarin, sitting at his window upstairs, overheard them!

"Be gone, Chang! And never let me see your worthless, low-bred face in my garden, in my mansion or in my realm! How dare you talk of marrying her?"

So Chang was banished and Li-chi's tears fell, just as the willow began to shed its leaves into the glassy lake.

But under cover of night, Chang crept back to the garden of the mandarin and called Li-chi's name in a whisper. "Come away with me to my home which is farther than Anyang or Pekin and stands among the hills of Li." She climbed down to him through the branches of the orange tree.

"We will hide in the gardener's hut on the island in the centre of the lake," said Li-chi. "My father will never think of looking for me in so foul a place. Tomorrow night, when he has stopped searching, we will escape!"

So it was that they crossed their beloved bridge hand in hand, and hid all night in the gardener's hut, where earwigs crawled and spiders wove their webs, and silk worms glowed and wet slugs nestled.

All next day they heard the noise of the search. The mandarin's servants searched the mansion from top to bottom. They searched the pavilions and the flowery grove. They even shook the last leaves from the weeping willow, while the mandarin himself roamed his garden swearing vengeance on Chang.

Evening came. Huddled on their island in the gardener's hut, Li-chi and Chang kissed and prepared to make their escape.

But as they stepped on to the bridge to cross from island to shore, there, barring their way, stood the mandarin, a huge whip in his hand. "There is no escape!" he shouted. "I've trapped you, treacherous Chang. Prepare to die!"

Li-chi gave a cry of terror. "Oh Chang, Chang, what have I done to you? There is no way off the island but across this bridge!"

On and on, the mandarin came, cracking his whip. It seemed certain that Chang would be beaten to death. "Jump, Chang!" cried Li-chi. "Jump with me into the water. For if we cannot be together in life, we shall be together in death!" And hand in hand they leaped to certain death in the waters below the bridge!

Great was the power of the

mandarins of old China. But greater still was the power of the gods! Looking down from the mountain tops, the gods loved Li-chi and Chang for their faithfulness and courage.

Just as the mandarin's whip slashed the air where they had been standing, Li-chi's white arms were turned into the loveliest of feathers, and Chang's body dissolved into dove's down.

The gods had transformed the lovers into two turtle doves!

They flew far, far away — out of sight and out of reach of the cruel old mandarin. It is said that they built a nest, far away, among the hills of Li. And now all the world knows their story. For the potters of China painted it, in saddest blue, on finest porcelain, and sold their wares far across the seas — farther even than Pekin, Anyang or the distant lands of Tibet.

Peter
and the
Mountainy
Men

Long, long ago, in the mountains of Switzerland, there lived a rich miller who was very mean. Even when people were starving and pleading for food, he would not help them.

One cold winter's day there was a knock on the mill door. "What do you want?" barked the miller.

"Please, sir, could you give me just one small bag of flour?" pleaded a tiny man dressed in a red cap and little green suit. "We need it so badly."

"Buzz off!" shouted the miller. "I've no time for beggars!"

As the dwarf began his long walk back to the mountains, he met a young boy carrying a bag of flour in his arms. It was Peter, the miller's son.

"Take this," he whispered, "but don't let my father know I've given it to you."

The dwarf took the bag and tucked it inside his coat. "Thank you, young sir," he said. "I'll not forget your kindness." Then he continued on his way.

One spring morning, several months

later, Peter was fishing in a lake up in the mountains when he felt a strong pull on his line. He tugged and tugged, until, suddenly, a little figure appeared from out of the water. It was the dwarf!

"Why, if it isn't the miller's son!" he said, drying himself on a huge leaf. "I've been having my annual bath in honour of the Great Day."

"Great Day?" asked Peter.

"Didn't you know? Today's our Great Day of Feasts and Sports. Why don't you come and join us? It's great fun and there's heaps to eat!"

The dwarf dived into the long grass, and pulled out his red cap and green clothes. Then he led the way through a hollow tree trunk to a huge cave in the hillside. This was where all the mountainy people — the elves, the dwarfs and the fairies — make their home.

In the huge cave hundreds of little folk dressed in gaily coloured clothes sat at long, low tables munching cakes, jellies and ice-cream. And there were great bowls of fruit and tall jugs of juice.

The dwarf banged on the table for silence. Immediately the chattering and music stopped.

"Dwarfs, goblins and fairies, this is Peter, the boy who gave us the bag of flour last winter. He's here as my special guest for the Great Day!"

The mountainy people clapped and cheered, as Peter sat down at the head table and began to eat, and eat . . . and eat. But, long before he had finished, the games began.

There was hurdling over the benches and pole-vaulting over the tables. The leprechauns played shinty, and a big crowd gathered to watch the darts match played with goose feathers. Skittles were played with a marble and big fir cones, and for javelin-throwing they used long twigs.

Peter was invited to join in the fun, but refused politely. "I don't really think it would be fair. After all, I'm so much bigger than you . . . and stronger."

"I wouldn't count on that," said a goblin — and he lifted up the bench, Peter and all!

The miller's son sat entranced as the elves rode bareback on racing mice, and the fairies used little wooden boats to race down a stream running through the cave. And all the time there were dwarfs doing handstands and somersaults, sometimes for prizes but mostly for fun. Then, after a tug-of-war between the goblins and the

gremlins, everyone ran out to the top of the mountain and back — and fell down exhausted.

Peter picked his way through the tired little bodies, taking care not to step on the fairies' wings. He crept out of the cave and climbed up the tree trunk back to the lake.

Just as he picked up his fishing rod he heard a voice calling to him. "Wait, Peter, wait for me!" It was the mountainy man. "You're leaving without your presents."

"Presents? But it isn't my birthday."

"I know it isn't. I mean your thank-you presents. You gave us flour when we were starving, so please take this whistle in return for your kindness. Just blow it loudly three times and we'll bring you whatever you want."

Amazed at all he had seen, Peter could scarcely find words to thank the little man. "And this," said the dwarf taking a bag from inside his coat, "is a flour bag for your father."

As the sun was sinking, Peter reached the mill, gave his father the bag and told him that the dwarf had given it to him.

"You mean you sneaked out and gave one of my bags of flour to that little beggar?" shouted the miller. But then he peeped inside the bag . . . and found a hundred shining pearls, with a note:

We hope this makes you happy not sad,
Mountainy folk return good for bad.

The miller felt so ashamed he promised Peter that never again would he turn away anyone in need of help.

So, ever after that, when the first winter snow fell high on the mountains, all the little people visited their friends, the miller and Peter.

And they always found the miller's table laden with delicious food.

ANANSI AND THE FANCY DRESS PARTY

Anansi the spider-man scratched his head and sat down to have a good think. Like all the other animals, he had received an invitation to King Leo's fancy dress party. It was to be held at three o'clock that afternoon and a prize was to be given for the most unusual costume. But Anansi had a problem — he just could not decide what to wear.

"Rabbit and Bear are bound to turn up in something *really* special," he muttered. "I'll have to find an absolutely fantastic costume if I'm going to win that prize."

He scratched his head and thought very hard.

"I have it. I have a brilliant idea. I'll go dressed up as a knight in a suit of armour."

Anansi set to work straight away. He took a wheelbarrow to a scrap-heap down the road and collected a huge pile of metal. There was an old wash-tub which had a hole in the bottom and would fit snugly round his body. There was a saucepan to put on his head and two square baking tins to wear on his feet. And there were lots of tin cans which he could use to cover his arms and legs by knocking out the bottoms and tying them together with bits of string.

By lunchtime the suit was ready for Anansi to try on. It looked perfect — but it had one drawback.

"I'll never be able to walk to the party in this suit," he thought. "It's much too heavy. What shall I do?"

He soon came up with the answer. He would put the suit in his wheelbarrow and push it to the field where the party was going to be held. He would hide the suit in some bushes and put it on just before three o'clock. Everyone would be so surprised that he would be certain to win the competition.

Anansi hid the suit and returned home feeling sure that nobody had seen him. He did not realise that at the very moment he pushed his suit into the hedge, Rabbit and Bear were standing on the other side.

"It really is excellent," said Bear. "It might have won the competition if we hadn't found it."

"Poor Anansi," said Rabbit. "How disappointed he'll be when he finds it's gone."

A few hours later Anansi returned to the hedge. He had decided that he would be too hot if he wore the armour over his clothes, so all he had on was a small sheet tied round his waist.

He had a nasty surprise when he saw that the suit was gone — but he quickly guessed what had happened to it. "Only Rabbit and Bear would have played such a mean trick," he thought, and he ran off to Rabbit's burrow.

He arrived in time to see the two friends struggling to get into their costume. It was an imitation donkey's skin. Rabbit was having trouble making his ears lie down so that he could put on the donkey's head. And Bear was finding it very difficult to squeeze himself into the donkey's back legs.

"Oh do hurry up," said Rabbit. "We're going to be late for the party."

"I'm trying to hurry," said Bear. "And anyway, there's no need to panic. We can take a short cut across Farmer George's carrot field."

When Anansi heard this he had a wonderful idea.

"I'll get my own back on those two rogues," he thought. "I'll tell Farmer George about the very strange donkey that's about to enter his field."

A few minutes later a very odd-looking beast stumbled into Farmer George's carrot field. The front legs were much shorter than the back legs and the head was only a few inches above the ground.

"Just look at all those lovely carrots," Rabbit said, smacking his lips.

"You know I can't see anything," said Bear. "What's more, we really are going to be late if you don't get a move on."

At that moment Farmer George crept up behind the strange donkey. He was holding a big, strong stick and he was very angry.

"That Rabbit and Bear are always after my carrots," he thought. "Well now, I'll teach them a lesson they'll never forget." And he brought the stick down hard on the donkey's back.

"Ow," yelled Bear as he stumbled forward. "What was that?"

"Don't push," said Rabbit. "I'm going as fast as I can."

Then Farmer George struck again. He struck the donkey's back so hard that Bear collapsed on top of Rabbit.

"What's the matter with you?" gasped Rabbit as he tried to wriggle away from Bear. But then he got a great blow on his head — and Bear got yet another on his back.

"Help!" cried the two friends together. "We're being attacked by a madman."

As the blows came thick and fast, they frantically struggled to get away. The donkey was a writhing mass of limbs until finally the skin split in two and the friends ran as fast as they could across the field.

Anansi had never seen anything so funny. Bent over with laughter, he walked away — heading straight for the field where the party was being held! The next thing he knew was that a lot of animals in fancy dress were all laughing at him.

"Just look at Baby Anansi," Monkey

cried. "Where's his dummy?"

"He's too young to be here on his own," chortled Snake.

"You'd think he'd be cold in just his nappy," sniggered Pig.

Anansi hung his head in shame. All the animals thought his sheet was a nappy! How he wished he had never thought of making a suit of armour.

But then King Leo spoke. "Nobody but you, Anansi, would think of dressing as a baby. Your costume is so unusual, you deserve to win the competition."

The other animals agreed. After all, the spider-man had given them their best laugh for weeks.

SCARLET BRACES

Now if there's one thing the people of Ireland know about, it's the ways of the Irish leprechaun. They will tell you that the leprechauns make all the shoes and boots the fairies wear. They will tell you that every leprechaun has a pot of gold hidden away in a secret place. And they will tell you, if you see a leprechaun, never to take your eyes off him or he will disappear before you look back again.

That is why, when Pat Fitzpatrick went out and about each day, he was always saying to himself, "If I ever see a leprechaun, I won't take my eyes off him till he gives me his pot of gold."

Pat might have been a better boy if he had spent more time helping his mother dig potatoes and less time looking for leprechauns and pots of gold.

Still, all that searching paid off. One fine day Pat caught sight of a little man — no bigger than his own hand — sitting on a toadstool, sewing a pair of fairy boots. Pat bit his lip and stood very still. "I won't take my eyes off him, so I won't. Not till he's made me the richest boy in all Ireland!"

Quietly, Pat crept through the grass until he was close enough to reach out and grab the leprechaun in his fist.

"Got you! Now, where's your pot of gold?"

give me any of your nonsense, now," he said. "I shan't let you go until you show me your pot of gold."

The leprechaun writhed and struggled until he wriggled one hand free and could point over Pat's shoulder. "Look, boy, and be quick! Your cow's in the corn!"

Pat very nearly turned his head to look. But, just in the nick of time, he saw it was a trick. "You'll have to do better than that," he laughed, shaking the leprechaun. "I am not taking my eyes off you till I have your pot of gold safe in my hands!"

Then the leprechaun burst into pitiful tears. "Ah, you're a cruel, heartless boy, so you are. Anyone can see that. Here you stand talking of gold when your own house is burning down and your mother inside it!"

"What!"

"Oh! Would you frighten a poor creature half to death?" cried the leprechaun, and his little heart pounded beneath Pat's fingers. "What's that you say about gold? I don't know of any gold, or anything about it at all!"

Pat squeezed the leprechaun a little tighter, never once looking away. "Don't

"Since you won't take your eyes off me, I am unable to tell you a lie. My pot of gold's buried below this particular thistle. But I'm thinking you'll need a spade if you're to dig it up."

"Oho, I see your trick," Pat jeered, squeezing the leprechaun until the little chap's eyes bulged. "You think I'll never find this one thistle again among so many!" So he untied the scarlet braces from round the leprechaun and tied them round the thistle instead, to mark it. Then he pushed the leprechaun deep into his pocket.

In his horror, Pat very nearly dropped the leprechaun and ran home. Just in the nick of time, he saw it was a trick, and shook the leprechaun until the poor little fellow turned as green as his own coat.

"All right, all right," the leprechaun spluttered at last. "I'll tell you where to find my pot of gold."

"No you won't, you'll show me the very spot," said Pat. And taking off his scarlet braces, he tied them to the leprechaun like a lead to a dog.

The magical little cobbler led Pat to the top of a hill. Thousands upon thousands of thistles grew in every direction. He stopped beside one thistle that looked exactly like every other.

But the very moment he lost sight of him, the leprechaun changed into thin air and was gone.

Pat did not mind. He ran home as fast as his legs would carry him, and fetched a spade. It was so heavy that he had to drag it behind him all the way back to the hill. "Thought he could trick me, eh?" he panted. "Well, he didn't reckon on the cleverness of good old Pat Fitzpatrick!"

Puffing and blowing, he stopped at the top of the hill to mop his forehead. And there was a sight in front of him that made his jaw drop.

A pair of scarlet braces dangled from every thistle in sight, as far as the eye could see — thousands upon thousands of scarlet braces. There was no more hope of recognising the leprechaun's thistle than of finding one particular drop of water in the whole of the Irish Sea.

So, if you ever chance to see a leprechaun, and you've a mind to steal his pot of gold, you had better keep a sharp eye on the little fellow . . . and remember the story of Pat Fitzpatrick and his scarlet braces!

The Mango-Seller

There was once a prince in India who was very, very lonely. In his search for a wife he had travelled from the most northern borders to the most southern tip of India. But although he had met many rich and beautiful young women — any one of whom would have happily agreed to marry him — he had always returned to his palace alone.

His courtiers could not understand it. "But your majesty," they would say. "You have been introduced to the richest and most beautiful women in India. Why are you still not married?"

"The answer is simple," the prince would reply sadly. "I have not yet met a woman I could love."

Each morning the prince sat by a window overlooking the market square. Occasionally a troupe of acrobats or jugglers brought a smile to his lips, but usually he just sat in gloomy silence listening to traders and shoppers haggling over prices.

Then, one day, he heard a voice which rang out clear and sweet above all the others. "Mangoes, fresh mangoes! Who'll buy my lovely, ripe mangoes?"

Rousing himself, the prince leaned out of the window and saw a girl carrying a basket of mangoes on her head. She was very poor, and her clothes were in tatters, but a smile lit up the prince's face as he watched her walking gracefully through the jostling crowd.

unhappy for the rest of my life if you do not agree to marry me."

"But of course I will agree," Rashida replied — and the prince immediately ordered preparations for a magnificent wedding.

"Surely, your majesty," the courtiers said. "You don't really mean to marry a common mango-seller?"

But the prince refused to listen to them. And within a few days he was a married man.

At first the couple were very happy. But then, as the months passed, Rashida began to change. When the prince told her how beautiful she was and how much he loved her she would just shrug impatiently and say, "I know, I *know*. You've told me the same thing every day since we were married." And she never, never smiled.

"How beautiful she is," he sighed. "And although she holds her head up high, how meek her eyes are. I must meet her straight away."

He ordered a courtier to run after the mango-seller and bring her to the palace.

"What is your name?" he asked eagerly.

She was so in awe of the prince that she dared not look at him and stood gazing at the floor.

"Rashida," she whispered.

"Please let me see your eyes, Rashida. They made me fall in love the moment I saw you. They told me your beauty hasn't made you proud, that you are indeed the woman I've been looking for. I will be

The months turned to years and Rashida became a woman whom the prince could hardly recognise. She was still beautiful, but she was also proud and haughty. She expected the highest compliments to be paid to her every day and all her commands to be obeyed instantly. She was cold and unfriendly to everyone — including her husband.

Desperate to see her smile again, the prince decided to celebrate their third wedding anniversary with a great banquet. At the end of the meal he took a mango from a platter of fruit and presented it to Rashida. She stared at him in disbelief.

"Surely you don't expect me to eat *that?*" she said.

The prince's eyes clouded with anger. "You've obviously forgotten you were once happy to sell mangoes in the market-place. Perhaps it's time you sold them again and forgot your proud, new ways."

"If you no longer love me I will not stay in your palace another moment," replied Rashida proudly. "I shall make sure you will never have to see me again." And without another word she swept out of the room.

In the weeks that followed the prince tried hard to keep himself busy so that he would not have time to think about Rashida. But it was no good. He could not forget the moment when he had first seen her and fallen in love.

One day he was riding through the market-place of a city, far from his palace, when he heard a clear voice. "Mangoes, fresh mangoes! Who'll buy my lovely, ripe mangoes?"

He recognised the sweet tone immediately, and he turned round to see Rashida walking through the crowd with a basket of mangoes on her head. She looked poor and hungry, but as beautiful as ever. He leaped off his horse and ran after her.

"Oh Rashida," he called. "How I regret the day I sent you away. Will you come back with me to my palace?"

Rashida lowered her eyes in shame. "Can you ever forgive me for being so proud?" she asked.

"I have already forgiven you," the prince said gently.

"Then I will gladly come with you." And, smiling, Rashida took the prince's hand and kissed it. Never again was she to lose her smile and become cold and proud. And she and the prince lived happily together for the rest of their lives.

the CREATURES with Beautiful Eyes

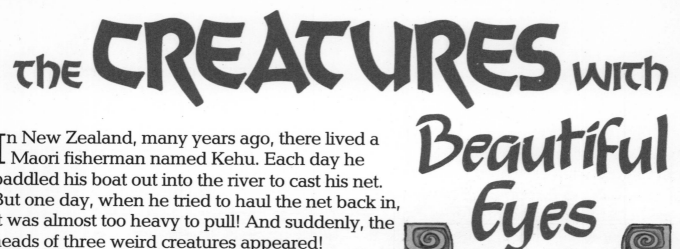

In New Zealand, many years ago, there lived a Maori fisherman named Kehu. Each day he paddled his boat out into the river to cast his net. But one day, when he tried to haul the net back in, it was almost too heavy to pull! And suddenly, the heads of three weird creatures appeared!

The first was a scaly merman, with a long, curling tongue; the second a slippery, fat snake; and the third a wriggling, giant lizard whose open mouth was filled with razor-sharp teeth. Kehu grabbed his spear to kill the creatures — but then he saw they were all staring at him, with soft, pleading eyes. They were the most beautiful eyes he had ever seen.

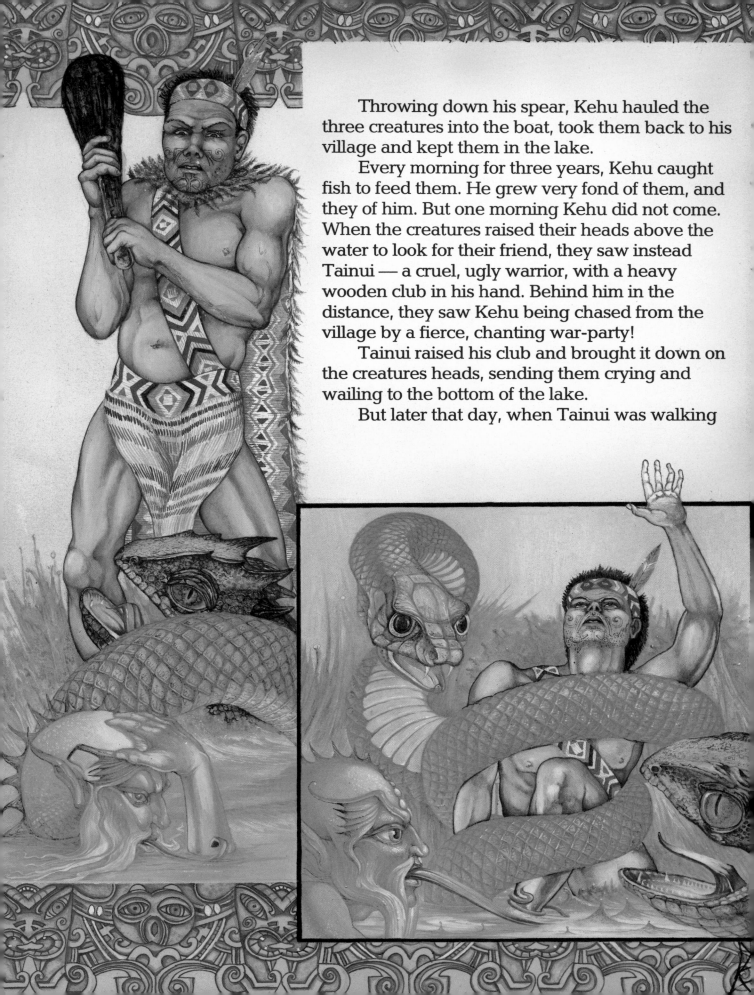

Throwing down his spear, Kehu hauled the three creatures into the boat, took them back to his village and kept them in the lake.

Every morning for three years, Kehu caught fish to feed them. He grew very fond of them, and they of him. But one morning Kehu did not come. When the creatures raised their heads above the water to look for their friend, they saw instead Tainui — a cruel, ugly warrior, with a heavy wooden club in his hand. Behind him in the distance, they saw Kehu being chased from the village by a fierce, chanting war-party!

Tainui raised his club and brought it down on the creatures heads, sending them crying and wailing to the bottom of the lake.

But later that day, when Tainui was walking

by the lake, a long, curling tongue coiled itself around his leg and pulled him into the water. Then the fat, slippery snake wrapped itself around his body, and squeezed and squeezed him. And then the lizard opened its mouth full of razor-sharp teeth, and prepared to bite him in two.

"Stop! Don't kill him!" called a familiar voice.

The creatures looked round to find their friend Kehu racing towards the lakeside with a band of villagers. They had just driven off the raiding war-party, and were heavily armed with clubs and daggers and spears. Kehu dragged Tainui out of the water, and tied him to a nearby tree.

Tainui's life was spared. But for the rest of his days he was kept there by the lake and forced to catch fish — for the creatures with beautiful eyes.

The Great Big Hairy Boggart

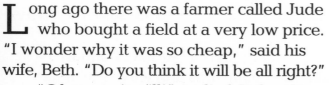

Long ago there was a farmer called Jude who bought a field at a very low price. "I wonder why it was so cheap," said his wife, Beth. "Do you think it will be all right?"

"Of course it will!" replied Jude. "It's good land. And to think it's mine. All mine!"

"*Mine*, you mean!"

Jude and Beth turned round and were amazed to see a great big hairy boggart, standing only a few yards away. He had bloodshot eyes and a nose as round and red as a beetroot. Long, fleshy ears poked through his hair, which stood up like a hedgehog's prickles. He had a set of whiskers as tangled as a hawthorn bush.

The boggart's clothes were in tatters and his trousers were held up with old rope. His hairy knees and elbows showed through ragged tears and worn-out holes. And he had the longest arms you have ever seen, with fists as big as turnips.

"Get off my land!" he shrieked, waving his arms about like a windmill.

"*Your* land?" said Jude.

"That's what I said. *My* land, and my boggart father's land before me, and his father's before that."

"You must be joking," said Jude. "I paid good money for this land and I signed the deeds."

"You just get yourself off it!" yelled the boggart. "I was here first!" And he began to jump up and down in a rage.

"Well *I'm* here now!" said Jude. "And *I* own it."

105

They stuck their chins out and glared angrily at each other. But neither of them would give way. Then Beth said: "Perhaps I've got the answer. You plant the crop, Jude, and the boggart can reap it. Then we can all have the harvest."

"Hmm, all right," said the boggart.

Jude did not see why he should do all the work and then give half his crop away. But Beth waved a hand to silence him.

"So which half of the crop do you want, boggart, the tops or the bottoms?"

"You what?"

"Do you want what grows *above* the ground or what grows *under* it. One or the other. Be quick. Make up your mind."

"Oh, I'll take the tops," chuckled the boggart. "You can keep the roots."

So Jude and the boggart shook hands on the bargain.

"Fine!" said Beth as she walked home with Jude. "All you have to do now is plant potatoes."

So Jude ploughed his land and planted potatoes. He hoed the weeds and watched the bushy green plants come up. When harvest came the great big hairy boggart returned to the field and demanded his share of the crop.

"There you are," said Jude. "The tops are all yours. Lovely potato plants just right for . . . well, I'm sure you'll find some use for them."

"You little rogue!" roared the boggart. "You miserable cheat! That's not fair! Why, I'll, I'll . . ."

"A bargain is a bargain, boggart. Now take the potato tops and leave me alone."

"Hmmph!" The boggart was fuming with anger. "I'll get even with you next time."

"What do you want next year then, tops or bottoms?" asked Beth.

"Bottoms, of course. *You* can keep the

"Now, now!" said Jude. "A deal's a deal."

"All right, farmer Jude, you win this time. But next year we'll both have the top of the crop. And you'll plant *wheat*. When harvest time comes we'll *both* reap it. *You* start from the north end of the field and *I'll* start from the south. We keep what we cut."

Jude looked at the boggart's long arms and he knew that he would be able to cut the wheat much faster than he could.

"No, no deal," said Jude.

"It's either that or a fight to the death!" growled the boggart, and he thrashed his hairy arms above his head and stamped his huge feet.

"What a terrible sight!" laughed Jude. "Please — don't let's fight. I wouldn't want to hurt a boggart!" So they shook hands on the deal and the boggart went away sniggering.

Jude told Beth about the bargain. "He's got such strong arms! He'll cut ten times as much wheat as I can. He's beaten us this time, I'm afraid."

Beth thought for a minute. "Suppose that some of the wheat grew with tougher stalks than the rest," she said. "Then one scythe would get blunt much quicker than the other." And she told him her plan.

"Oh, that's it!" said Jude. "I'm glad the boggart doesn't have a wife as clever as you!"

tops next time!" And the boggart stomped off.

"Now what shall we do?" asked Jude.

"Plant barley, my dear. Let the boggart make what he can out of barley roots!"

So, after Jude had dug up all his potatoes, he planted his field and sowed barley seed. He rolled the land and watered it, and when the spring came young green shoots appeared. By harvest time, when the great big hairy boggart arrived for his share of the crop, the field was a swaying carpet of gold.

"There it is," said Jude. "I'll have the tops and you can have the roots."

The boggart screamed with rage. "You've cheated me again, you little shrimp. Why I'll, I'll . . ."

Jude ploughed the land and planted the wheat seed, then he watched the crop grow tall and golden. Just before the harvest he bought some thin iron rods and crept out to the boggart's end of the field in the middle of the night. He stuck the rods into the ground among the stalks of wheat.

Harvest day came and the great big hairy boggart arrived, carrying a scythe in each of his huge hands. Jude started cutting the wheat from the top end of the field, and the boggart started from the other. Jude swung his single scythe in steady, sweeping strokes and the golden wheat fell down all around him. But the boggart cut and hacked and sweated and swore, and then he stopped.

"The weeds in the wheat down this end seem mighty tough!" he shouted.

"No trouble up this end!" called Jude.

The boggart was too stupid to notice the iron rods. So he sharpened both scythes and went on hacking at the wheat. Eventually he stopped again, mopping his forehead. "I'm tired out with cutting these weeds."

"Really?" said Jude. "That's funny. I'm still as fresh as a daisy."

The boggart tried again, swinging his scythes in all directions, but with each stroke they got more blunt and chipped. Finally he threw them down in a rage.

"You can keep your useless land!" he yelled at Jude. "It's more trouble than it's worth." He strode off over a hedge and vanished down the road into the distance. And the great big hairy boggart never bothered Jude and Beth again.

Child of the Sun

There is a very old tale that tells of a man and his wife who lived on a small island off the west coast of Canada. They were very lonely, for they had no children and no-one else lived on the island.

One evening, when the sky was the colour of seagull's feathers, the young woman sat alone on the seashore looking out across the water.

"If only we had children, they could play on the sand with me and I wouldn't be so lonely," she said.

A kingfisher nearby was diving in the mouth of the river with his young.

"O kingfisher," said the young woman. "I wish I had children like you."

Then, to her amazement, the kingfisher replied: *"Look in the sea-shells! Look in the sea-shells."*

The next evening, when her husband was away fishing, the woman sat again on the beach looking out to the sea. She saw the seagull bobbing up and down on the waves with her brood of young gulls.

"O seagull," the young woman sighed. "I do wish I had children like you."

And the seagull replied: *"Look in the sea-shells. Go and look in the sea-shells."*

Then suddenly she heard a cry from behind her. It came from a large sea-shell lying in the sand. Picking it up, the woman looked inside and saw a tiny boy, crying as hard as he could.

She carried the baby home and looked after him. He soon grew into a strong little boy. One day the boy said to the young woman: "I must have a bow made from the copper bracelet on your arm."

The woman smiled. And to please the little boy she made a tiny bow and two tiny arrows.

The next day the boy went out hunting with his bright new bow. And after that he went out hunting every day, bringing back geese, ducks and all sorts of small sea-birds.

As he grew older, the boy's face turned a deep golden colour, brighter than the shine of his little golden bow. And when he sat on the beach, gazing out to sea, the weather was always calm and there were strange bright lights on the water.

One day a huge storm blew over the ocean and the sea was so rough that the

fisherman could not go out in his boat. And before long he and his wife and the little boy had no more fish to eat.

Then the boy said, "Let me go out in the boat with you, Father, because I will conquer the Storm Spirit."

The man did not want to go out in the boat as the sea was so violent, but the boy continued to plead so much that he finally agreed.

Together they set out across the stormy sea. They had not gone far when they met the Storm Spirit blowing in from the southwest, where the great winds live.

Tossing the little boat this way and that,

the Storm Spirit blew and blew like a wild monster. But for all his blowing he could not turn the small boat over. The boy guided it through the waves, and soon the sea was calm all around them.

Then the Storm Spirit called his friend Mist of the Sea to come and hide the water, for he knew that when the Mist came down the man and the boy would soon be lost.

When the man saw Mist of the Sea spreading across the water he was terrified. He was more afraid of Mist of the Sea than any of his many enemies on the waters.

But the boy said, "Don't be afraid. He will not harm you when I am with you."

When the Mist of the Sea saw the boy sitting in front of the little boat, and smiling, he disappeared as quickly as he had arrived. There was nothing else the Storm Spirit could do so he turned away in anger, and the sea was safe again.

As they set off for home the boy taught his father a magic song, which they sang to the fish. When they heard it, the fish swam into the nets and by evening the boat was loaded up with a fine catch.

"Tell me the secret of your power," said the father.

"I can't tell you yet," replied the boy.

The next day the boy went out with his copper bow and arrows and shot many birds. When he got home he skinned them and hung up the skins to dry. Then he covered himself in the skins of plovers, rose into the air and flew above the sea. Below him the sea was a dull grey, like the colour of his wings.

After flying round the island, he

came down. He took off the plover skins, and put on the feathers of blue jays, and again soared up into the air. The sea beneath him immediately turned to a blue like the blue of his wings. Again he flew round the island and returned to the beach.

This time he put on the skins of robins, which had a reddish golden colour from their breast feathers. As he flew high over the sea the waves below him reflected the colour of fire. Bright gleams of light appeared on the ocean, and the western sky shone a golden red.

When he came back to the beach the boy said to his mother: "I am the Child of the Sun. It is time for me to go now, and I shall leave this island for ever. But I shall appear to you often in the western sky when the sun shines bright at the end of the day. When the sky and sea at evening are the golden colour of my face you will know that the next day will be fine, and there will be neither wind nor storm.

"And though I have to leave you I will give you special powers. Wear this magic robe and if you ever need me you can let me know by sending little white signals to me, so I can see them from my home in the west."

The boy gave his mother the magic robe and flew off to the west, leaving the fisherman and his wife very sad.

Now, when the woman sits in the sand and loosens her magic robe, the wind starts blowing and the sea becomes rough. And the more she loosens it, the more the storm rages.

But in the autumn, when mists roll in from the sea and the evening sky is dull, she remembers the boy's promise. Taking the tiny white feathers from the breasts of birds, she tosses them into the wind. Turning to snowflakes, they fly off to the west to tell the boy that the world is grey and lonely and that it longs for the sight of his golden face.

Then, after the sun has fled, the boy appears, and the sky is set on fire and the sea is sprinkled with golden light. And the people of the Earth know that there will be no wind the next day and the weather will be fine. Just as the Child of the Sun promised them, long ago.

PETRUSHKA

The bells were ringing out all over Moscow. A mighty pealing chorus echoed far across the city. It was Shrove Tuesday, the day of the great carnival.

Admiralty Square was packed with people, and there were entertainers everywhere — strongmen lifting massive bar-bells, bareback riders on nimble little ponies, sword-swallowers and fire-eaters, jugglers and dancers.

Most popular of all was a brightly coloured tent where a Showman was introducing his puppet show.

"The show you are about to witness, ladies and gentlemen, is a spectacle unmatched in all the Russias!" declared the Showman, his black eyes glinting beneath his fur hat. "The puppets you will see today are quite unlike any you have ever seen! They will come alive before your very eyes!"

With a flourish, the Showman flicked aside the curtain to reveal three magnificent puppets: the Moor, a dashing Moroccan prince; the Princess, a delicate ballerina; and Petrushka, a wicked-looking sailor.

"They're not alive!" came a hoarse shout from the back of the crowd, where a fat merchant was winking at two gypsy girls. "Tell us another one. Hah!"

But with a withering glance, the Showman pulled from his deep pocket a tiny silver flute and touched each puppet in turn upon the shoulder.

Instantly, they sprang to their feet, and as the Showman played a lively tune they danced and twisted about on the little stage.

At the end of the dance, the crowd cheered with delight — and with a loud guffaw, the merchant threw a pile of rouble notes high into the air! The gypsy girls jumped to catch them, but the Showman silenced everyone with a long, low note from the flute.

The puppets stood as if bewitched. Then the Showman began playing a slow, mysterious tune and the Moor stood proudly at one side of the stage, his hands on his hips. The Princess stood in the centre, smiling radiantly, and Petrushka fell to his knees, as if pleading with her.

"The ugly sailor Petrushka loves the Princess," said the Showman. "But she rejects him."

The ballerina turned to the Moor and took his arm. They strolled together at the edge of the stage, looking deep into each other's eyes. Then, Petrushka, snarling like a tiger, pulled out a cudgel and ran across the stage. He tried to attack his rival, but the Moor bravely stepped in front of the Princess and knocked the cudgel from the sailor's hand.

Petrushka crawled back across the stage, then turned and begged for mercy. But the ballerina took the Moor's arm and walked with him to the centre of the stage. Ignoring poor Petrushka, they hugged each other and bowed deeply to the crowd.

"Thus the Moor marries the Princess and the sailor becomes their servant," boomed the Showman, and he swept the curtain back across the stage. "The last show will be at four o'clock." Then he walked through the crowd, collecting coins in his fur hat.

The Showman sat down on a bench behind the theatre, and counted his money. It had been a good day, all right! Five shows already, and plenty of coins in the hat! He gave a deep, throaty chuckle, and closed his eyes for a nap.

But behind the curtain, in their dressing rooms, the puppets were stirring.

Petrushka the ugly sailor was in tears. "How I hate that Showman," he cried. "Why did he make me so ugly, and the Princess so beautiful? If only I was handsome, like the Moor, or I could dance like him! Then perhaps she might love me instead!" He jerked to his feet and took a few, awkward steps towards the stage. "I must learn to dance, I must! Then I will kill the Moor, and marry the Princess."

At that moment Petrushka noticed the ballerina watching him from her room. She danced towards him on the tips of her toes, as graceful and as delicate as a bird. Petrushka's heart pounded, and he tried desperately to dance beside her, but it was no good. He tripped over his feet and fell to the floor.

The ballerina soon got bored with watching his clumsy efforts. So she danced away again, along the stage.

The Moor in his dressing room was practising with his scimitar in front of a mirror. He strode manfully up and down, and cut and slashed and lunged. But when the ballerina danced in, the Moor sprang to attention. He clapped merrily

and stamped his feet as she glided towards him. Then they spun around together in a wild, Eastern dance.

Suddenly Petrushka burst in. He had been watching them from the stage and he could not bear to see his beloved ballerina dancing with the Moor. "Take your hands off my Princess!" he shouted. And he charged at the Moor, brandishing his cudgel.

Outside the theatre, a crowd was gathering for the last show of the day. The golden domes threw long shadows across the square, but many people had stayed late to see the famous puppet show. The merchant was back again, with his two gypsy girls, and there was even a performing bear with his trainer! They all gathered in a semi-circle and waited patiently while the Showman recited his speech:

"Ladies and gentlemen, the puppets you will see today are unlike any you have ever seen. They will come alive before your . . ."

But, at that moment, the curtains burst open behind the Showman's back. Petrushka leaped down from the stage and ran away full pelt across the square. Behind him rushed the Moor, in a furious rage, waving the scimitar above his head. As the crowd turned in astonishment, Petrushka slipped and fell. Down came the scimitar in a great, flashing arc, and Petrushka lay deadly still, face down in the snow.

"They're alive!" shouted the merchant. There's been a murder!"

But the Showman snatched up the Moor and Petrushka, and shook and slapped them. A trail of sawdust trickled down from Petrushka's face. "There you are," he whined. "Just puppets. But there'll be no more shows today, ladies and gentlemen."

As the crowd drifted away, the Showman thrust the two puppets in through the back of the theatre and closed the tent. Then he walked off to a tavern, shaking his head gloomily.

Later that night he returned to the theatre. He drew back the curtain, and peered inside. There was the ballerina, sleeping in her room.

The Moor sat cross-legged on the stage, quietly polishing his scimitar. On the floor lay Petrushka, broken and torn.

"What was that?" gasped the Showman. Something was moving in the darkness above the theatre. He looked up and saw in the moonlight — the ghost of Petrushka, dancing in the air. It shook its fist and scowled at the Showman.

"You made me ugly!" it snarled. "You made a fool of me! But now it's my turn, I'm free of the body you made for me. Now I can dance as well as anyone. Watch me! My love for the ballerina has made my spirit delicate and free. But my ugliness will haunt you for the rest of your days!

And his laughter echoed in the frosty air.

THE FARMER, THE TOMT AND THE TROLL

— WANTED —

There was once a Swedish farmer who was so mean that no-one would work for him. In the end he was forced to advertise for a Tomt — which is what Swedish dwarfs are called — to gather in the harvest.

Only one Tomt applied for the job. He was three feet tall, very old and very wrinkled. And his long white beard trailed all the way down to the ground.

"I may not look much, but I can work very fast," said the Tomt. "If you pay me well, I'll cut all your corn in a single night."

"You're hired," replied the farmer, and he crossed his fingers behind his back. "Two bags of gold will be ready for you at eight o'clock tomorrow morning."

Before the Tomt set off for work, he sang a song:
"I shall scythe and I shall reap
While the farmer's fast asleep.
In the morning, draw my pay,
And hop, skip, jump, I'll be away."

All night long the little Tomt toiled and by seven o'clock in the morning the entire wheat crop had been harvested and neatly stacked in the barn.

"Finished at last," said the Tomt, and at eight o'clock he knocked on the farmer's door.

He knocked once, he knocked twice, he knocked three times — but there was no reply.

He bellowed through the letter-box. He threw pebbles at the shutters. At last the farmer poked his head out of a window and shouted, "What's all the fuss about?"

"I want my pay," said the Tomt.

"Well, you can't have it now — come back this time next year and I'll see what I can do." And he slammed the window shut.

The poor little Tomt was so furious at being cheated that he went off to a nearby hill to plan his revenge.

It was a very odd shaped hill and when the Tomt reached the top, he found he was standing on the end of a huge nose.

"Good heavens," he said to himself. "This isn't a hill at all, it's a Troll! And I have been trampling all over him with my dusty shoes!"

"I don't mind," said the Troll. "It's lonely up here and I like a little conversation now and then."

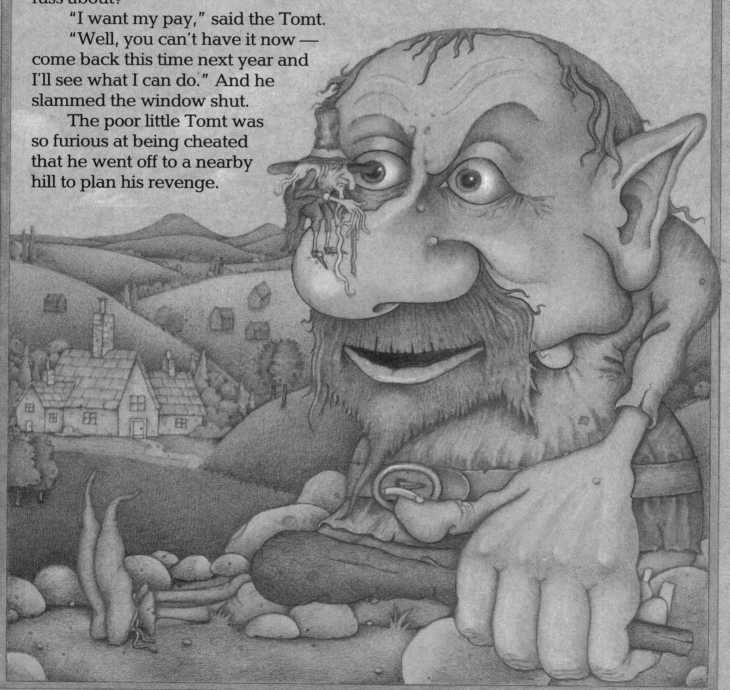

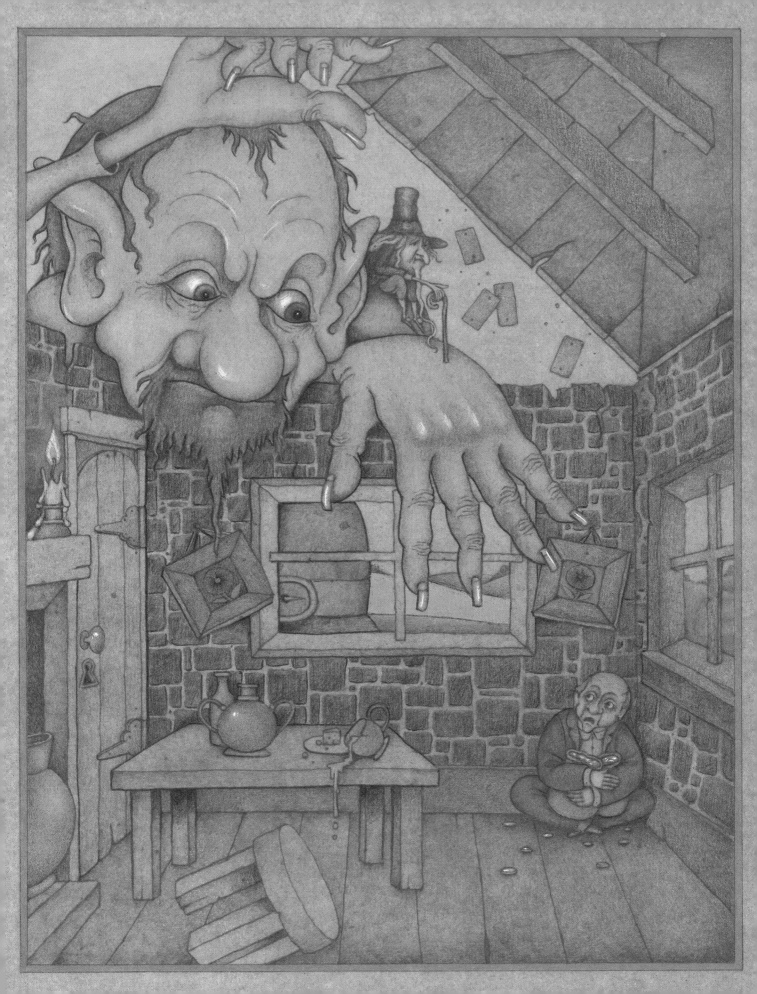

So the Tomt told the Troll his sad story, and the Troll was absolutely furious. "Fancy cheating a poor little Tomt like you."

Then the Troll had an idea. "Let's visit the farmer together. I'm sure he'll pay up when he sees you've got a big brother like me." So they marched off to the farm.

The farmer was eating his dinner when he heard a loud knock at the door. "Who's there?" he growled.

The Tomt shouted through the letter-box, "Will you please pay me my wages. Get the money and be prompt. Do not make me wait for ages. It's bad luck to cheat a Tomt."

"Go away," growled the farmer. "I won't pay." Then he looked out of the window and saw a gigantic Troll armed with a wooden club standing outside.

"If you don't pay, you'll lose your hay," said the Troll, and with a mighty puff he blew all the farmer's haystacks into the pond. Then he leaned on the roof until it creaked and said very quietly, "Pay or I'll crack your chimney stack."

But frightened as he was, the farmer was too mean to hand over any money, so the Troll lifted the roof and peered inside.

The farmer was sitting on the kitchen floor, hugging his bags of gold. With a trembling hand, the farmer held up one bag, "Will this do?" he asked.

"Not enough," said the Tomt.

"Two bags?"

"That's right," said the Tomt, grabbing his wages.

"And one for me," said the Troll, stuffing another bag of gold into his pocket.

Then the Tomt climbed on to the Troll's huge shoulders and they marched away, singing a victory song:

"Tomts and Trolls must stand together,
If they are to get their way.
Now we're off to spend the money
On a seaside holiday."

ABDULLA and the GENIE

W here the golden sands of Arabia touch the deep blue sea, there once lived a poor fisherman called Abdulla. Every day he would stand on the beach for hours and hours, casting his net into the water.

Most days he was lucky and caught a few fish. But on one particular day he seemed to have no luck at all. With his first throw of the net he hauled in a heap of slimy green seaweed. With his second throw he brought in a pile of broken plates and dishes. And with his third throw he dragged in a mass of black, sticky mud.

"Wait a minute," he thought as the mud oozed out of the net at his feet. "There's an old bottle. I wonder what's in it."

Abdulla tried to take out the tight-fitting stopper. After he had tugged and pulled at it for some time it suddenly popped out, and a flurry of dust shot out of the bottle. The dust quickly changed to smoke. And then the smoke changed colour, and the colours began to make a shape — first a face, then a body. And the figure grew bigger and bigger . . . and bigger. In just a few seconds an enormous genie was towering over the frightened fisherman.

"*Free at last!*" boomed a voice louder than thunder. "Free after all these years! And I'm going to eat you up!"

Abdulla clutched at his head. "Why, why? What have I done to you?"

"I'll cut you into tiny pieces!" roared the genie, swatting a flock of birds as they flew past his shoulder.

"Don't do that, Master Genie," pleaded Abdulla, falling to his knees. "I didn't mean to disturb you. *Please* don't kill me!"

"I'll feed you to the fish, in little mouthfuls!" bellowed the genie, drawing out a massive curved sword and almost touching the fisherman's nose with it.

"Have mercy!" cried Abdulla. "What harm have I done?"

"*Silence!*" bawled the genie. And he shouted so loudly that a nearby volcano began to erupt. "Be silent and I shall tell you my reason for killing you."

And without moving his sword from Abdulla's face, the genie started his story . . .

"The Great Sultan Suleiman shut me up in that bottle as punishment for the wicked magic I worked in his kingdom. He squashed me into that horrible glass prison like a whale squeezed into an egg. Then he threw it into the sea.

"I slopped about in the dark silence for centuries. All I could hear was my own breathing. All I could feel was my own heartbeat. All I could hope for was to be fished out and set free by a fisherman.

"For the first thousand years I called out: *'Let me out! Let me out! Somebody let me out and I will grant you three wishes.'* But nobody heard me, and nobody set me free.

"For the next thousand years I called out: *'Let me out! Let me out! Somebody let me out and I will give you the whole of Arabia for a present.'* But nobody heard me, and nobody set me free.

"For the next thousand years I kept quiet and thought to myself: *'If ever I get out of this terrible bottle I shall kill the first man I see — and every man I see after him!'*"

"But Sultan Suleiman died nearly three thousand years ago!" cried Abdulla.

"Exactly!" snapped the genie. "Is it any wonder that I'm in such a bad temper?" And he gave a great shriek, and the water boiled around his ankles. He lifted his great sword and it flashed in the sun, and cut a cloud to ribbons overhead. Then he peered down to enjoy for one last time the look of terror on the little fisherman's face.

But instead of looking scared, Abdulla was standing with his hands on his hips, his head to one side, and a broad grin on his face.

"Now, now genie," he said calmly. "Stop pulling my leg and tell me where you *really* came from."

The ground shook as the genie took a deep breath. *"What?* You worm! You little beetle! *Prepare to die!"* And he lifted his sword over his head.

"Oh, come on. You must be joking. What a tall story. Tell me where you *really* came from. I was busy emptying this old bottle I pulled in and I didn't see you creep up on me."

"What? You ant! You earwig! I came out of that bottle! And I am going to kill *everybody."*

"Dear, oh dear," sighed Abdulla. "Didn't your mother ever warn you not to tell lies, especially big ones? I can see the size of that *bottle* and I can see the size of

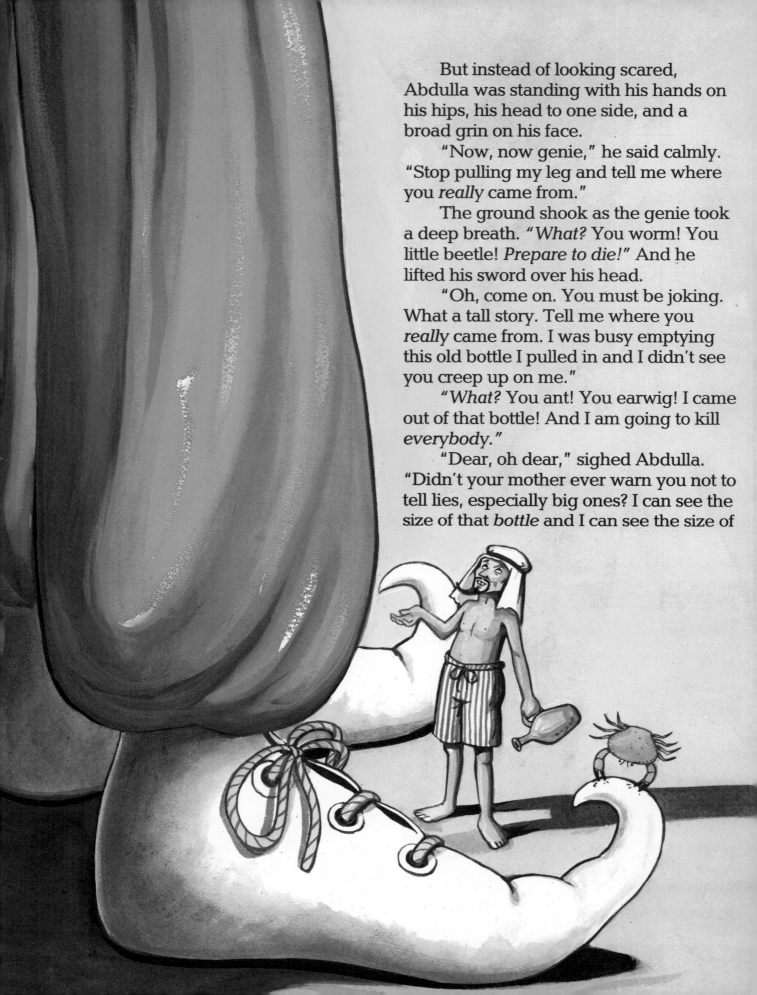

you. You no more came out of that bottle than I did." And Abdulla made a great show of trying to get his foot down the bottle's narrow neck.

"You cockroach! You . . . you . . ." The genie's bottom lip began to tremble. "I *did* come out of that bottle. I *did!*"

"Pah," scoffed Abdulla as he turned to walk away. "Then *prove* it."

The hairs on the genie's grubby chest began to bristle and he thumped on the sky with rage. Then, after a few moments thought, he melted like a piece of butter into all the colours of the rainbow. The colours dissolved away and a shower of smoke and ash tumbled out of the sky and poured back into the little bottle.

"*See!*" said a funny hollow voice from inside. "I told you so."

Quick as a flash, Abdulla snatched the stopper out of his pocket and jammed it into the neck of the bottle. He pushed and turned and turned and pushed until it was wedged fast.

"Hey! Let me out, you little worm! Let me out right now!"

"Oh no," said Abdulla, laughing. "You can stay in there for another thousand years if you're going to be so unpleasant."

"No! Please, no! I'll grant you three wishes if you let me out again. Open this bottle at once, you ant!"

Abdulla leaned back and with all his strength threw the bottle as far as he could out to sea. "I'll give you all Arabia!" shrieked the genie as the bottle flew through the air. Then the bottle fell — *plop* — back into the water. And no sound could be heard except for the waves breaking gently on the shore.

Later that day Abdulla returned to the beach and put up a notice. It read: '*Beware of the genie in the bottle. No fishing.*' Then he rolled up his net and moved to a new stretch of the beach.

The Fairies' Cake

"Oh, we'll turn you into a tree."

"I don't want to turn into a tree," thought Lucy. So she said to the fairies, "How can I make a cake without flour? You'd better fly to my kitchen and fetch me a bag of flour."

So the fairies flitted over to the croft where Lucy lived, and flitted back with a bag of flour.

Lucy shook her head. "How can I make a cake without eggs? You'd better fly to my hen-house and fetch me half a dozen eggs."

So the fairies flew over to the hen-house, and flew back with half a dozen eggs.

"But how can I make a cake without sugar?" said Lucy to the fairies. "You'd better hurry to my cupboard and fetch a bag of sugar." So the fairies fluttered over to the croft and found in the cupboard a bag of sugar, and

There was once a young lady called Lucy who baked the best cakes in the whole world. One day she was stolen away by the fairies, who locked her up in the kitchen in Fairyland. "Make us a cake!" they all demanded. "A big, gooey, crumbly, creamy cake with icing!"

"And what will become of me when I've done baking?" asked Lucy.

128

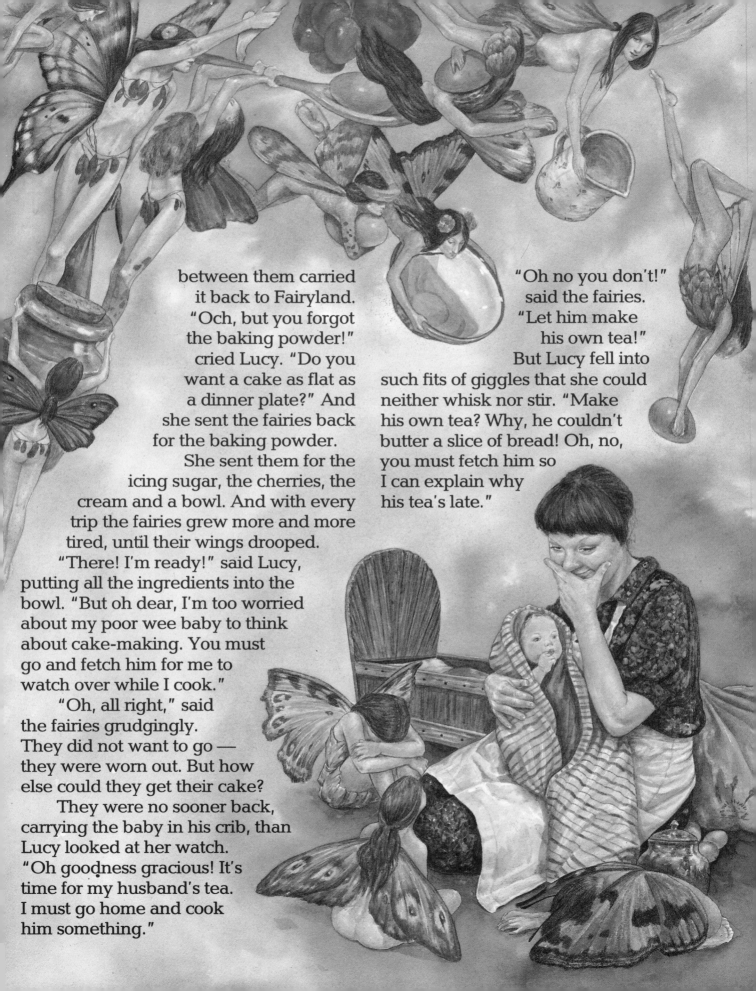

between them carried it back to Fairyland. "Och, but you forgot the baking powder!" cried Lucy. "Do you want a cake as flat as a dinner plate?" And she sent the fairies back for the baking powder.

She sent them for the icing sugar, the cherries, the cream and a bowl. And with every trip the fairies grew more and more tired, until their wings drooped.

"There! I'm ready!" said Lucy, putting all the ingredients into the bowl. "But oh dear, I'm too worried about my poor wee baby to think about cake-making. You must go and fetch him for me to watch over while I cook."

"Oh, all right," said the fairies grudgingly. They did not want to go — they were worn out. But how else could they get their cake?

They were no sooner back, carrying the baby in his crib, than Lucy looked at her watch. "Oh goodness gracious! It's time for my husband's tea. I must go home and cook him something."

"Oh no you don't!" said the fairies. "Let him make his own tea!" But Lucy fell into such fits of giggles that she could neither whisk nor stir. "Make his own tea? Why, he couldn't butter a slice of bread! Oh, no, you must fetch him so I can explain why his tea's late."

a cake more than ever. So they folded their wings across their backs and walked all the way over to Lucy's croft, and carried back the cat and the dog.

"Now. At last I'm ready to bake the cake," said Lucy. "But where's the oven?"

"Oven?" The fairies began to grizzle. "Do you need an oven?"

Lucy laughed and her husband laughed, too. "Of course I need an oven!"

So the fairies crawled over to the croft and staggered back under the gigantic weight of the cast-iron kitchen range.

While they were gone, Lucy said to her husband, "Sing!" And she said to the cat, "Yowl!" And she said to the dog,

So the fairies flapped over to the croft — and flapped back with Lucy's husband. Then they sat back to back on the floor to catch their breath.

"Did you lock up the cat and dog before you left?" Lucy asked her husband sharply — though she winked an eye as she spoke.

"Er . . . er, no, I-I didn't have time."

"What? The dog and cat not locked up? Why, they'll scratch the house to pieces! You fairies will have to fetch them here — no two ways about it!"

The fairies could hardly bring themselves to get up off the floor. But they were so hungry that they wanted

"Ssh! Oh shush! Stop!" shrieked the fairies, covering their ears. "Go away, *please!*" they cried, pulling their pillows over their heads.

"Very well," said Lucy. "But only if you promise to fetch my oven home tomorrow morning at the latest."

Then her husband picked up the baby in his crib, and Lucy picked up the cat, and the dog followed on behind. They walked home to a meal of cold pork pie and toasted crumpets.

"Bark!" And she said to the baby, "Cry!"

The door flew open, and in came the oven. The fairies set it down, then sprawled on their little fairy beds, exhausted.

But the man was singing.
And the cat was yowling.
And the dog was barking.
And the baby was crying.

But Lucy, though she had narrowly escaped being turned into a tree, felt sorry for the fairies with no-one to bake them cakes. So when they brought back her oven, the first thing she did was to bake a big, gooey, crumbly, creamy cake with icing on top, and she left it outside the door. And do you know what? Next morning it was gone.

Good King Wenceslas

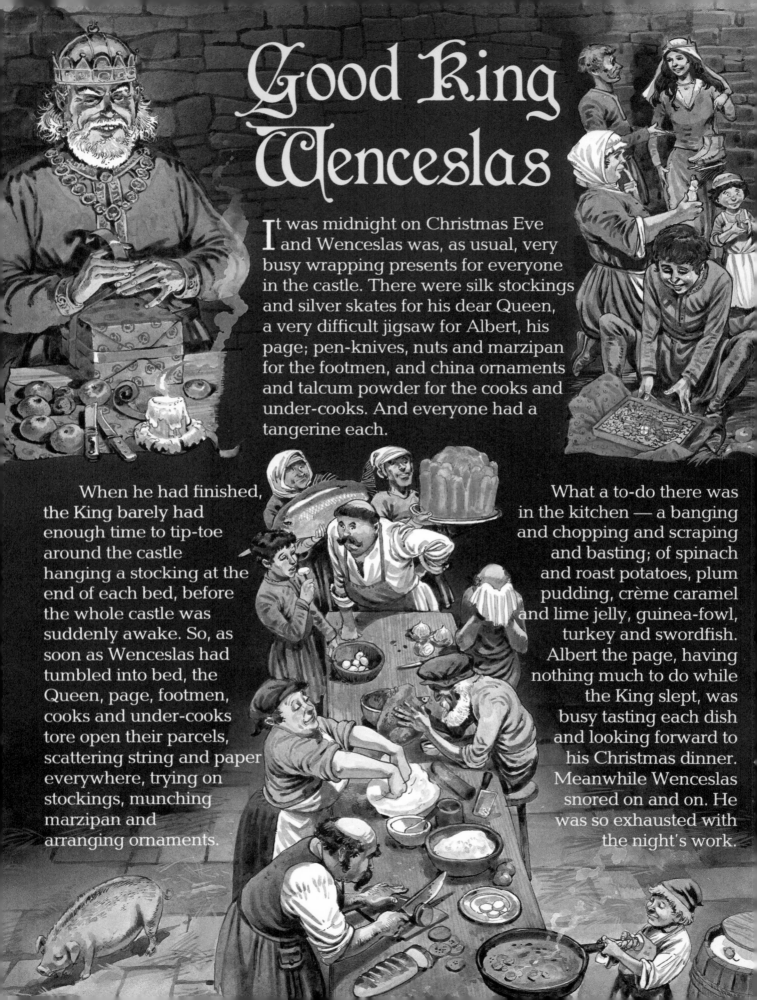

It was midnight on Christmas Eve and Wenceslas was, as usual, very busy wrapping presents for everyone in the castle. There were silk stockings and silver skates for his dear Queen, a very difficult jigsaw for Albert, his page; pen-knives, nuts and marzipan for the footmen, and china ornaments and talcum powder for the cooks and under-cooks. And everyone had a tangerine each.

When he had finished, the King barely had enough time to tip-toe around the castle hanging a stocking at the end of each bed, before the whole castle was suddenly awake. So, as soon as Wenceslas had tumbled into bed, the Queen, page, footmen, cooks and under-cooks tore open their parcels, scattering string and paper everywhere, trying on stockings, munching marzipan and arranging ornaments.

What a to-do there was in the kitchen — a banging and chopping and scraping and basting; of spinach and roast potatoes, plum pudding, crème caramel and lime jelly, guinea-fowl, turkey and swordfish. Albert the page, having nothing much to do while the King slept, was busy tasting each dish and looking forward to his Christmas dinner. Meanwhile Wenceslas snored on and on. He was so exhausted with the night's work.

The Queen came in, kissed him, and gave him a pair of slippers embroidered with his initials. The King mumbled, "Charming my dear," and went back to sleep again. Albert, tiring of his hard work in the kitchen, came in and gave him a goldfish he had won at the summer fair. Wenceslas murmured, "Delightful, my boy," and went back to sleep again.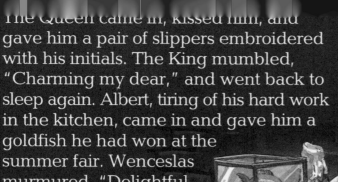

He slept on and on, while the Queen, the page, the Court and guests from far and wide ate their sumptuous Christmas dinner. Glasses were filled and refilled, crackers pulled and balloons popped. Then the court orchestra struck up and the entertainment started.

Six important guests from Italy performed a juggling act while standing in a human pyramid, the King of France rather unexpectedly danced the tango with his pet bear, and a Druid from Wales recited a long poem. This made everyone feel suddenly very weary, and the singing, laughter and shrieks of excitement died away. The whole party nodded quietly in their seats, the candles flickering low as the evening went on and. darkness fell outside, where silent snow had already fallen.

Wenceslas, meanwhile, woke up refreshed and full of energy. He stretched, jumped out of bed and pushed his feet into his new slippers. Walking over to his bedroom window, he leaned out, sniffing the frosty air with pleasure. Down below he spied an old man collecting firewood.

"I wonder who that can be, wandering about outside on a night like this?" thought Wenceslas, and he went to look for Albert, who with the Queen and all the guests was still snoozing peacefully in the dining-hall.

Wenceslas shook his page gently by the shoulder. "Wake up, my boy, I need your help," he whispered.

Albert rubbed his eyes, yawning and protesting. "Oh sire, I've eaten too much. I feel so-o-o sleepy."

"Come, my boy, we've got work to do. But first tell me — do you know who that old man might be I've just seen collecting firewood outside the castle?"

"Oh yes, sire, that's an old man who lives miles away at the bottom of the mountain.

He often comes over here collecting firewood."

"Hmm. Well now, fetch me as many pine logs as you can carry." Albert disappeared and Wenceslas went round the table, filling a basket with chunks of meat and decanters of wine.

When the page returned, staggering under a pile of logs, Wenceslas said, "Now, put on your warmest cloak. We're off to visit our friend at the bottom of the mountain and give him a surprise."

"But, sire, it's *freezing* outside!"

Wenceslas silenced him with a mild frown. "Just remember, not everyone has had the splendid Christmas that *you* have, or has a warm castle to live in."

And off they tramped in the snow. Wenceslas carried the logs, and Albert followed behind with the basket of food. They put it all down at the old man's door. "There," said Wenceslas. "Now at least he'll have a bit of Christmas dinner, and enough wood to last a few days."

Then they retraced their footsteps to the castle, Albert still following behind. As he walked, he felt the strangest thing — he did not know if it was because of all the food and wine he had had, but as he followed in his master's footsteps, his body tingled all over with warmth as though it was the finest summer's day.

"I wonder if anyone would believe me if I told them. No, they'd probably laugh at me. I think I'll just keep it to myself." And Albert snuggled up contentedly inside his cloak as the lights of the castle came into view.

Good King Wenceslas looked out,
On the Feast of Stephen,
When the snow lay round about,
Deep and crisp and even;
Brightly shone the moon that night,
Though the frost was cruel,
When a poor man came in sight,
Gathering winter fuel.

"Hither, page, and stand by me,
If thou know'st it, telling,
Yonder peasant, who is he?
Where and what his dwelling?"
"Sire, he lives a good league hence,
Underneath the mountain,
Right against the forest fence,
By Saint Agnes' fountain."

"Bring me flesh, and bring me wine,
Bring me pine logs hither;
Thou and I will see him dine,
When we bear them thither."
Page and monarch forth they went,
Forth they went together
Through the rude wind's wild lament
And the bitter weather.

"Sire, the night is darker now,
And the wind blows stronger;
Fails my heart, I know not how,
I can go no longer."
"Mark my footsteps, good my page,
Tread thou in them boldly;
Thou shalt find the winter's rage
Freeze thy blood less coldly."

In his master's steps he trod,
Where the snow lay dinted;
Heat was in the very sod
Which the saint had printed.
Therefore, Christian men, be sure
Wealth or rank possessing,
Ye who now will bless the poor
Shall yourselves find blessing.

Molly Whuppie

Once upon a time, there was an old wood-cutter who had many children. Work as he might, he could hardly feed them all. One day he gave the three youngest a slice of bread and treacle each, and sent them into the forest to gather wood.

They went deep into the trees, and when they turned to go home, they had forgotten the way. They ate the bread and treacle and walked and walked until they were worn out and utterly lost. Then, just as it was getting dark, they spied a small and beaming light chinkling out from a window. So the youngest of them, who was called Molly Whuppie and was by far the cleverest, went and knocked. A woman came to the door and asked them what they wanted. Molly Whuppie said, "Something to eat."

"Eat!" said the woman. "Eat! Why, my husband's a giant, and soon as say knife, he'd eat *you*." But they were tired and famished, and Molly begged the woman to let them in. So at last the woman sat them at the table and gave them some bread and milk. Hardly had they taken a sup of it when there came a thumping at the door. No mistaking that — it was the giant come home.

"Ha! ha!" he said. "What have we here?"

"Three poor, cold, hungry, lost little lasses," said his wife. "You get to your supper, my man, and leave them to me." The giant said nothing, sat down and ate up his supper — but between bites he looked at the children.

Now the giant had three daughters of his own, and the giant's wife put all six of them into the same bed. For so she thought she would keep the strangers safe. But before he went to bed the giant, as if in play, hung three chains of gold round his daughters' necks, and three of golden straw round Molly's and her sisters'.

Soon the other five were fast asleep in the great bed, but Molly lay awake listening. At last she rose up softly and changed over one by one the necklaces of gold and straw. So now it was Molly and her sisters who wore the chains of gold, and the giant's three daughters chains of straw.

In the middle of the night the giant came tip-toeing into the room and, groping with finger and thumb, he plucked up out of bed the three children with the straw necklaces, carried them downstairs, and bolted them up in his great cellar.

Molly thought it high time she and her sisters were out of that house. So she woke them, and they slipped down the stairs together and out into the forest, and never stopped running till morning.

At daybreak, lo and behold, they came to another house. It stood beside a pool of water full of wild swans, and stone statues, and a thousand windows — and it was the house of the King. So Molly went in, and told her story to the King.

The King listened, and when it was finished, said, "Well, Molly, that's one

thing done and done well. But I could tell
another thing, and that would be better."
The King knew the giant of old, and he told
Molly that if she would go back and steal the
giant's sword that hung beside his bed, he
would give her eldest sister his eldest son for
a husband.

Molly smiled and said she would try.

So that very evening she muffled herself
up and made her way back through the
forest to the house of the giant. First she
listened at the window, and heard the giant
eating his supper. So she crept into the
house and hid herself under his bed.

In the middle of the night Molly climbed
softly up on to the great bed and unhooked
the giant's sword that was dangling from its
nail in the wall. Lucky it was for Molly this
was not the giant's fighting sword, but only
a little sword. It was heavy enough for all
that, and when she came to the door, it
rattled in its scabbard and woke up the giant.

Then Molly carried off the sword to the King, and her eldest sister married the King's eldest son.

"Well," said the King, when the wedding was over, "that was a better thing done, Molly, and done well. But I know another, and that's better still. Steal the purse that lies under the giant's pillow, and I'll marry your second sister to my second son."

Molly laughed and said she would try.

So she muffled herself up, and stole off through the forest to the giant's house, and there he was, guzzling as usual at supper. This time she hid herself in his linen cupboard. A stuffy place that was.

About the middle of the night, she crept out, took a deep breath, and pushed her fingers just a little bit between his two pillows. The giant stopped snoring and sighed . . . but soon began to snore again. Then Molly slid her fingers in a little bit further. At this the giant called out in his sleep.

Then Molly ran, and the giant ran, and they both ran, and at last they came to the Bridge of the One Hair, and Molly ran over. But not the giant, for over he could not. Instead, he shook his fist at her across the chasm in between, and shouted:

"Woe betide ye, Molly Whuppie,
If ye e'er come back again!"

But Molly only laughed and said:
"Maybe twice I'll come and see ye,
If so be I come to Spain!"

"Woe betide ye, Molly Whuppie,
If ye e'er come back again!"

But Molly only laughed and called back:
"Once again I'll come to see ye,
If so be I come to Spain!"

So she took the purse to the King, and her second sister married his second son. There were great rejoicings.

"Well, well," said the King to Molly, when the feasting was over, "that was yet a better thing done, and done for good. But I know a better yet, and that's the best of all. Steal the giant's ring for me, and you shall have my youngest son for yourself."

And his wife said, "Lie easy, man! It's those bones you had for supper."

Then Molly pushed in her fingers a little bit further, and they felt the purse. But as she drew out the purse, a gold piece dropped out of it and clanked on to the floor, and at the sound of it the giant woke.

Then Molly ran, and the giant ran, and they both ran. And they both ran and ran until they came to the Bridge of the One Hair. And Molly got over, but the giant stayed, for get over he could not. Then he cried out across the chasm:

Molly laughed and looked at the King's youngest son, frowned, then laughed again, and said she would try. This time, when she had crept into the giant's house, she hid beside the chimney.

At dead of night, when the giant was snoring, she stepped out and crept towards the bed. By good chance the giant lay on his back, with his arm hanging down out over the bedside, and it was the arm that had the hand at the end of it on which was the thumb that wore the ring.

First Molly wetted the giant's thumb, then she tugged softly and softly at the ring. Little by little it slid down — but just as Molly slipped it off the giant woke with a roar, clutched at her, gripped her, and lifted her clean up over his head.

"Ah-ha! Molly Whuppie!" says he. "Once too many is never again. Aye, and if I'd done the ill to you as the ill you have done to *me,* what would I be getting for my pains?"

"Why," says Molly, "I'd bundle you up in a sack, and I'd put the cat and dog inside with you, and a needle and thread and a great pair of scissors, and I'd hang you up on the wall, be off to the wood, cut the thickest stick I could get, come home, take you down, and beat you to a jelly. *That's* what I'd do!"

"Ha-ha-ha! And that, Molly," says the giant, chuckling to himself, "that's just what I'll be doing with you." So he rose and fetched a sack, put Molly into the sack, and the cat and dog besides, and a needle and thread, and a stout pair of scissors, and hung her up on the wall. Then away he went into the forest to cut a club.

When he was well gone, Molly, stroking the dog with one hand and the cat with the other, sang out in a high, clear, happy voice, "Oh, if only *everybody* could see what I see!"

"See, Molly?" said the giant's wife. "What do you see?"

But Molly only said, "Oh, if only *everybody* could see what I see. Oh!"

At last the giant's wife *begged* Molly to let her see what Molly saw. Then Molly took the scissors and cut a hole in the corner of the sack, jumped out, helped the giant's wife up into it, and, as fast as she could, sewed up the hole with needle and thread.

It was pitch black in the sack, so the giant's wife saw nothing, and she soon asked to be let out again. Molly never answered her, but hid behind the door.

Home at last came the giant, with a wood club in his hand. And he began to thump the sack with the club. His wife cried, "Stop, man, stop! It's me, man. Oh, oh, man, it's me, man!" But the dog barked and the cat squalled, and he did not hear her voice.

Then Molly crept softly out from behind the door. But the giant saw her. He gave a roar. And Molly ran, and the giant ran, and they both ran, and they ran and they ran and they ran — till they came to the Bridge of the One Hair. And Molly skipped over it. But the giant stayed, for he could not. And he cried out after her in a dreadful voice:

"*Woe betide ye, Molly Whuppie,*
If ever ye come back again!"
But Molly waved her hand at the giant and flung back her head:
"*Never again I'll come to see ye,*
Though so be I come to Spain!"
Then Molly ran off with the ring in her pocket, and she was married to the King's youngest son, and there was a feast that was a finer feast than all the feasts that had ever been in the King's house before, and there were lights in all the windows.

Lights so bright that all the dark long the wild swans swept circling in space under the stars. But though there were guests by the hundred from all parts of the country, the giant never so much as gnawed a bone!

The Swords of King Arthur

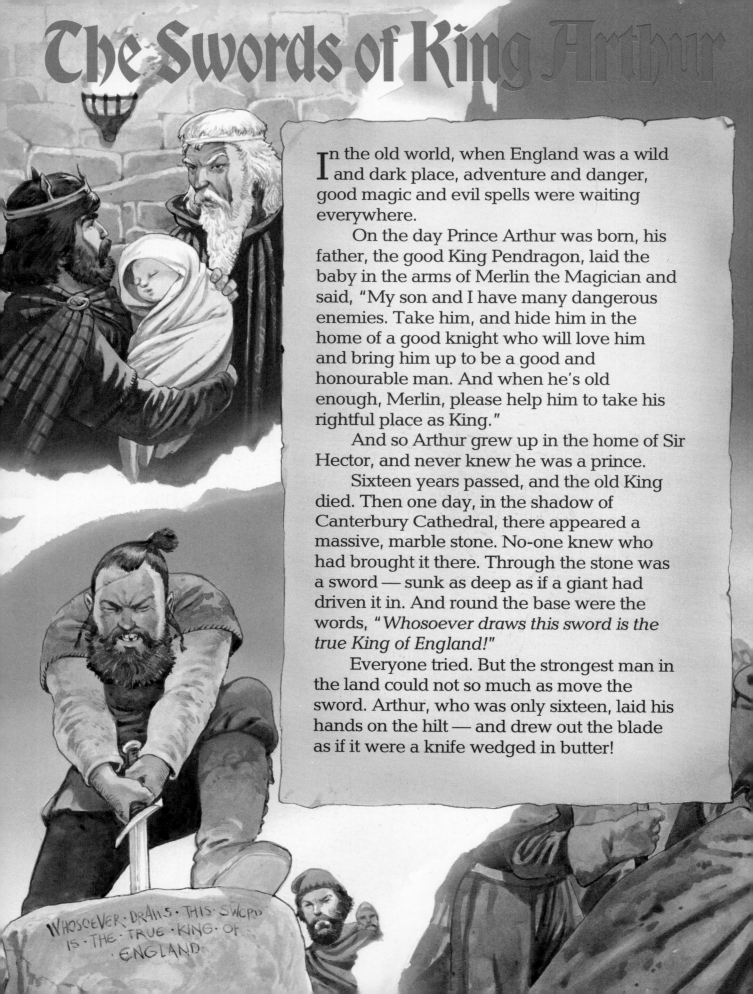

In the old world, when England was a wild and dark place, adventure and danger, good magic and evil spells were waiting everywhere.

On the day Prince Arthur was born, his father, the good King Pendragon, laid the baby in the arms of Merlin the Magician and said, "My son and I have many dangerous enemies. Take him, and hide him in the home of a good knight who will love him and bring him up to be a good and honourable man. And when he's old enough, Merlin, please help him to take his rightful place as King."

And so Arthur grew up in the home of Sir Hector, and never knew he was a prince.

Sixteen years passed, and the old King died. Then one day, in the shadow of Canterbury Cathedral, there appeared a massive, marble stone. No-one knew who had brought it there. Through the stone was a sword — sunk as deep as if a giant had driven it in. And round the base were the words, *"Whosoever draws this sword is the true King of England!"*

Everyone tried. But the strongest man in the land could not so much as move the sword. Arthur, who was only sixteen, laid his hands on the hilt — and drew out the blade as if it were a knife wedged in butter!

WHOSOEVER·DRAWS·THIS·SWORD·
IS·THE·TRUE·KING·OF·
ENGLAND.

Only then did Merlin show himself to Arthur and to the astonished crowds. "Take the throne, Arthur, and rule wisely and well."

"But Merlin, sir, I'm only a boy! How can I be King of England?" begged Arthur.

"You are Prince Arthur, son of Pendragon. And it is written in the stars that you will be the greatest King of all!"

As soon as Arthur had been crowned, Merlin's magic and wisdom protected him. The ageless magician taught the boy the language of the animals, the healing power of herbs, and the skills of battle.

The people began to say, "Arthur may be only sixteen, but he's a good King — the best we remember — the best England has ever had."

Heroes and knights flocked to his court at Camelot. Arthur ordered a huge table to be placed in the Great Hall. There he sat and discussed the affairs of England with his knights — his Knights of the Round Table.

And because the table was round, no-one felt more important or less important than anyone else — not even the King had a place of honour. The Knights of the Round Table swore to help the weak and to drive all manner of evil out of the land.

One day, as Arthur and his men rode out from his castle, they met a young knight so badly wounded that he seemed likely to tumble off his horse. "What's this?" said Arthur. "Who did this to you, sir?"

"My name is Griflet. I come from fighting Pellinore the Giant. He's set up his tent in the river gorge, and says no-one may pass without fighting him. He's so strong, my lord King!" said the knight. "Stay away from him, I beg you!"

"No! By my sword, I won't! I'll be revenged on him for the hurt he's done you, Griflet. Men! Cover my shield and take the crown off my helmet. I'll fight Pellinore alone, and he'll never know he's fighting the King."

Riding to the river gorge, Arthur saw a pavilion ahead. Beside it grew a tree, and on one branch hung an enormous shield. Arthur banged on it with his sword. "Who goes there?" boomed a gigantic voice. Out rushed the tallest knight Arthur had ever seen, brandishing a huge lance.

"I forbid you to pass!"

"No man forbids me!" cried Arthur.

"Then we'll fight!"

Pellinore mounted and they rode at each other. Three times they charged. Three times Arthur's lance gouged into the giant's shield. But at the third charge, Arthur was flung from his horse.

He got up and drew his sword. Pellinore did the same, secretly admiring this brave, young knight whose shield bore no crest. Their swords clashed again and again.

The King weakened and Pellinore drove him backwards against the stump of a tree. Arthur tripped, and as he fell, Pellinore slashed at Arthur's sword with such fury that he smashed it to pieces.

"Kneel and beg for mercy!" cried Pellinore.

"Never! I'd rather die!"

"Then die, but before I kill you, let me see your face, for you fought bravely."

Pellinore tore off Arthur's helmet, and looked into his face. But he did not recognise the newly crowned King. He raised his sword to strike . . .

"Stay your hand!"

Someone stepped out from the trees. It was Merlin the Magician, Arthur's own teacher. Pellinore recognised Merlin at once — after all, the old man had been famous throughout England for a hundred years.

"Would you kill the King of England?" Merlin demanded.

Pellinore stared in horror. Then, in desperation, he said, "If this is the King, I *must* kill him — or he will have me killed when he gets back to Camelot!"

But as Pellinore's sword began to fall, Merlin pointed a long finger at the knight. His magic struck like a thunderbolt. Pellinore dropped to the grass and lay as still as a dead man.

Arthur struggled to his feet. "You should not have killed him, Merlin. He beat me in a fair fight."

Merlin put an arm round Arthur's shoulders. "He's not dead, my boy, just sleeping. And you won't send your knights to kill him, will you?"

Arthur sighed and shook his head. "No. But oh, Merlin, the sword I pulled from the magic stone is smashed to pieces."

Merlin only smiled. "Then we had better pay a visit to the Lady of the Lake."

He led Arthur along a winding path which led to a peaceful lake. It seemed deserted. Suddenly, an arm clothed in white silk appeared out of the waters of the lake. In its hand was a sword in a scabbard, and the hilt was studded with jewels. "Whose sword is that?" whispered Arthur.

"It can be yours if you choose — though one day you must give it back to the Lady of the Lake. It is her hand you see before you."

When they had rowed out to the heart of the dark waters, Arthur leaned out and took the sword from the pale hand of the Lady of the Lake. As soon as he grasped it, the arm slipped out of sight.

Back on the shore, Merlin said, "The sword has magic power. It will help you to conquer your enemies. But the scabbard is just as wonderful. While you wear it, you will never lose one drop of blood, no matter how badly you are wounded."

"Then I'll wear it always . . . and the sword I shall call by name — Excalibur!" As Arthur and Merlin rode away together, an echo rose from the reed-fringed lake. "Excalibur . . . *Excalibur* . . . EXCALIBUR!"

Armed with the magical sword Excalibur, King Arthur drove many invaders and evil knights out of England. But he had one enemy more deadly than all the rest — not an invading king or a murderous knight, but his own beautiful half-sister, Morgan le Fay.

Morgan was a sorceress, and her black magic was every bit as strong as the good magic of Merlin the Magician. She hated Arthur for fighting evil. And she hated Excalibur, the sword which made Arthur strong in battle and whose scabbard protected him from injury.

One day, Arthur was riding out from Camelot with one of the Knights of the Round Table — a Frenchman called Sir Accolon. "I shall show you the place where I received Excalibur from the Lady of the Lake," said Arthur, as their horses threaded their way down a tangled path to the shores of a lake. "But is this the same place?" Arthur wondered, for the lake seemed strangely different.

Moored at the end of a crumbling jetty lay a huge black ship. A veiled woman stood on the bow, beckoning to them through the lakeside mists, as if to say, "Welcome! Come aboard!"

Surprised and intrigued, the two men boarded the ship. And there they found a banquet waiting.

"Were you expecting us?" asked Arthur, as the woman ushered them to the table. "Where are your crew? Where have you sailed from?" But their hostess neither spoke nor lifted her veil. Instead she poured wine for them and filled their plates with the most delicious food.

Two hammocks hung at the end of the cabin. And after Accolon and Arthur had eaten, all they wanted was to climb into them and rest. The boat rocked. The hammocks swung. Both knights were asleep before the lakeside birds stopped singing.

When the morning sun shone in his face, Sir Accolon yawned and opened his eyes. He was lying in a walled garden, and a servant was offering him a sword. "Get up at once, Sir Accolon! King Arthur bids you fight the evil White Knight who is waiting in the Great Hall!" Sir Accolon shook his head sleepily. "Look!" cried the servant urgently. "He has sent me to you with his magic sword, Excalibur. With this you'll destroy the White Knight in a twinkling!"

"Well I'll . . . I'll put my armour on!" said Sir Accolon. "Tell the White Knight I shall fight him within the hour!"

Meanwhile, Arthur woke up and found himself not on the ship, nor in the walled garden but chained up in a dungeon. A woman's voice shouted through the door, "Get up! Get up, Arthur, so-called King. To win your freedom you must fight the Red Knight who's waiting in the Great Hall."

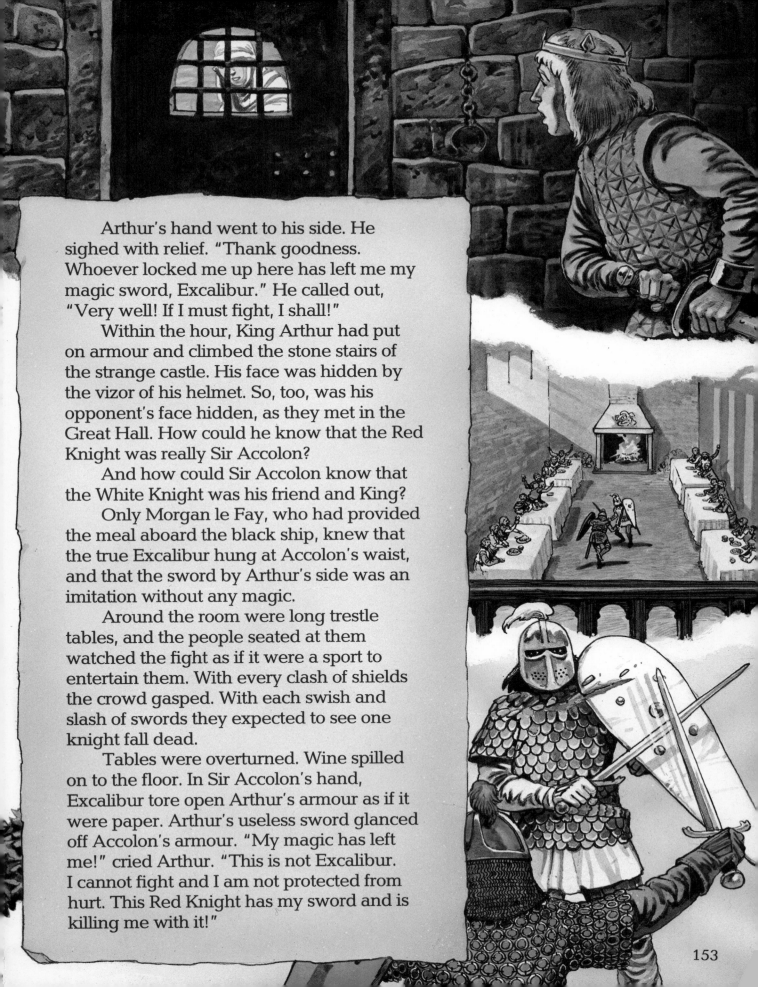

Arthur's hand went to his side. He sighed with relief. "Thank goodness. Whoever locked me up here has left me my magic sword, Excalibur." He called out, "Very well! If I must fight, I shall!"

Within the hour, King Arthur had put on armour and climbed the stone stairs of the strange castle. His face was hidden by the vizor of his helmet. So, too, was his opponent's face hidden, as they met in the Great Hall. How could he know that the Red Knight was really Sir Accolon?

And how could Sir Accolon know that the White Knight was his friend and King?

Only Morgan le Fay, who had provided the meal aboard the black ship, knew that the true Excalibur hung at Accolon's waist, and that the sword by Arthur's side was an imitation without any magic.

Around the room were long trestle tables, and the people seated at them watched the fight as if it were a sport to entertain them. With every clash of shields the crowd gasped. With each swish and slash of swords they expected to see one knight fall dead.

Tables were overturned. Wine spilled on to the floor. In Sir Accolon's hand, Excalibur tore open Arthur's armour as if it were paper. Arthur's useless sword glanced off Accolon's armour. "My magic has left me!" cried Arthur. "This is not Excalibur. I cannot fight and I am not protected from hurt. This Red Knight has my sword and is killing me with it!"

153

As he prepared to face death at the hands of the strange Red Knight, something caught Arthur's eye. Out on to the minstrel's gallery stepped an old man, tall and grey-haired. It was Merlin the Magician.

Merlin raised his gnarled old hand, knotted with purple veins. Suddenly, Sir Accolon's sword snaked and twisted out of his grip. Arthur sprang forward, seized the sword and lunged!

As Accolon fell, Arthur pulled off his helmet. "No! Accolon my friend! Who has done this?" he whispered. "Who has made me fight one of my own knights?" Then, clutching his beloved sword, he fell to the ground, weakened by his many wounds.

Merlin took Arthur to a convent where the nuns nursed him day and night. But so many were his wounds that they could not have saved his life but for Excalibur. In his right hand he held the sword by its jewelled hilt. And in his left he held the scabbard whose healing magic, little by little, made him well.

"He must have complete rest and quiet," said Merlin as he left the convent. "Let no-one visit him." The nuns promised they would not.

But when a beautiful and gentle-looking woman called one day and begged to visit Arthur, they could see no harm. "Please say 'yes'," pleaded the visitor. "Arthur is my brother, after all!" And so the scheming and envious Morgan le Fay was shown into the bedroom where Arthur lay sleeping.

His right hand was closed tight around the sword hilt. But the scabbard had slipped out of his other hand and lay on the pillow. Quickly, Morgan slipped it inside her cloak and hurried away.

The sound of her horse galloping away woke Arthur and he reached out to touch the scabbard which protected him from harm. It was gone. "Stolen!" he cried. "Somebody saddle me a horse! I must go after the thief!"

"But your Majesty!" exclaimed the nuns. "No-one has been here except your sister, Morgan!"

Realising the truth, Arthur rode after his treacherous sister, vowing to kill her for the evil trick she had played on him and on Accolon. His horse was fast, and he gained on Morgan with every mile.

She left the cart track and rode to the edge of a swampy lake. Taking the scabbard from under her cloak, she flung it into the oozing mud where it sank out of sight. "Never again shall my brother be protected from his injuries!" And all the beauty went out of her face for ever.

Closer and closer came Arthur. But Morgan the sorceress only swirled her cloak around her head and turned herself and her horse into a white bluff of rock. Arthur glanced at it as he rode past, but galloped on, and when, after many days, he had not found his sister, he rode home sadly to Camelot. But he vowed revenge, and swore that one day he would overcome the evil magic of Morgan le Fay.

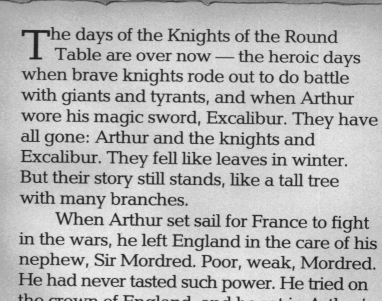

The days of the Knights of the Round Table are over now — the heroic days when brave knights rode out to do battle with giants and tyrants, and when Arthur wore his magic sword, Excalibur. They have all gone: Arthur and the knights and Excalibur. They fell like leaves in winter. But their story still stands, like a tall tree with many branches.

When Arthur set sail for France to fight in the wars, he left England in the care of his nephew, Sir Mordred. Poor, weak, Mordred. He had never tasted such power. He tried on the crown of England, and he sat in Arthur's seat at the Round Table. And he said to himself, "It's good to sit in the place of the King. But how much better it would be if I *owned* his crown and his chair and his castles!"

He gathered an army made up of all the worthless knights Arthur had banished or imprisoned. And the treacherous Morgan le Fay — half sister to the King — brought her black knights out of the Land of Blood to fight alongside Mordred.

The news reached France, and Arthur sailed home as fast as he could to do battle with Mordred and his sworn enemy, Morgan le Fay.

It was a terrible and terrifying battle.

Good knights and bad took each other's lives with sword and lance, mace and axe. Every one of Mordred's men was killed. Morgan the sorceress, seeing that the battle could not be won, fled the field and lived alone in her Realm of Blood, until both she and her magic withered and died.

At last, no-one on the battlefield was left alive but Sir Mordred, Arthur, and one young knight of the Round Table— the bold Sir Bedevere.

Mordred hammered at Arthur with his broadsword. But every blow from the King's magic sword Excalibur sliced open Mordred's shield. Arthur's shout rose above the clatter of weapons, "Die, you traitor! Excalibur is sharper than any sword that was ever drawn in battle!"

Mordred dropped on one knee. "Ah, but where is the magic scabbard to protect you from hurt? Didn't your own sister steal it from you? Isn't it lost for ever in the black ooze of a bog?" And jabbing one last time with his sword, he stabbed Arthur in the heart. As he did so he fell with his face to the ground and died.

Seeing the King stagger, Sir Bedevere ran to him across the battlefield and caught him in his arms. "I'll find Merlin, my lord! He'll make you well again," sobbed the young knight.

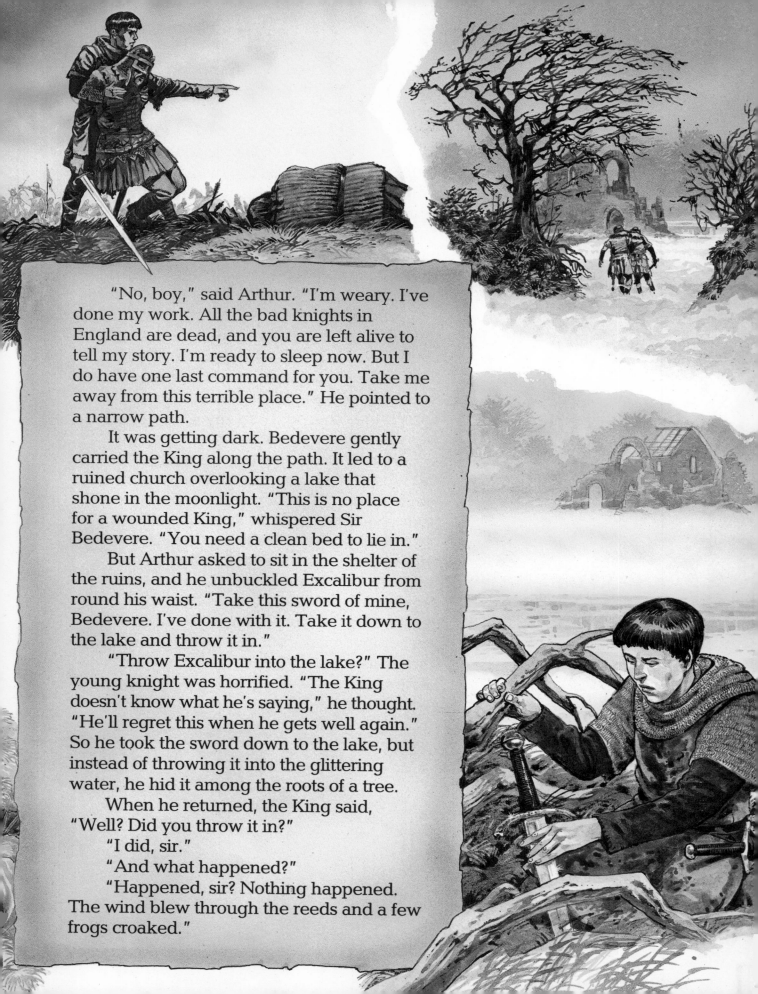

"No, boy," said Arthur. "I'm weary. I've done my work. All the bad knights in England are dead, and you are left alive to tell my story. I'm ready to sleep now. But I do have one last command for you. Take me away from this terrible place." He pointed to a narrow path.

It was getting dark. Bedevere gently carried the King along the path. It led to a ruined church overlooking a lake that shone in the moonlight. "This is no place for a wounded King," whispered Sir Bedevere. "You need a clean bed to lie in."

But Arthur asked to sit in the shelter of the ruins, and he unbuckled Excalibur from round his waist. "Take this sword of mine, Bedevere. I've done with it. Take it down to the lake and throw it in."

"Throw Excalibur into the lake?" The young knight was horrified. "The King doesn't know what he's saying," he thought. "He'll regret this when he gets well again." So he took the sword down to the lake, but instead of throwing it into the glittering water, he hid it among the roots of a tree.

When he returned, the King said, "Well? Did you throw it in?"

"I did, sir."

"And what happened?"

"Happened, sir? Nothing happened. The wind blew through the reeds and a few frogs croaked."

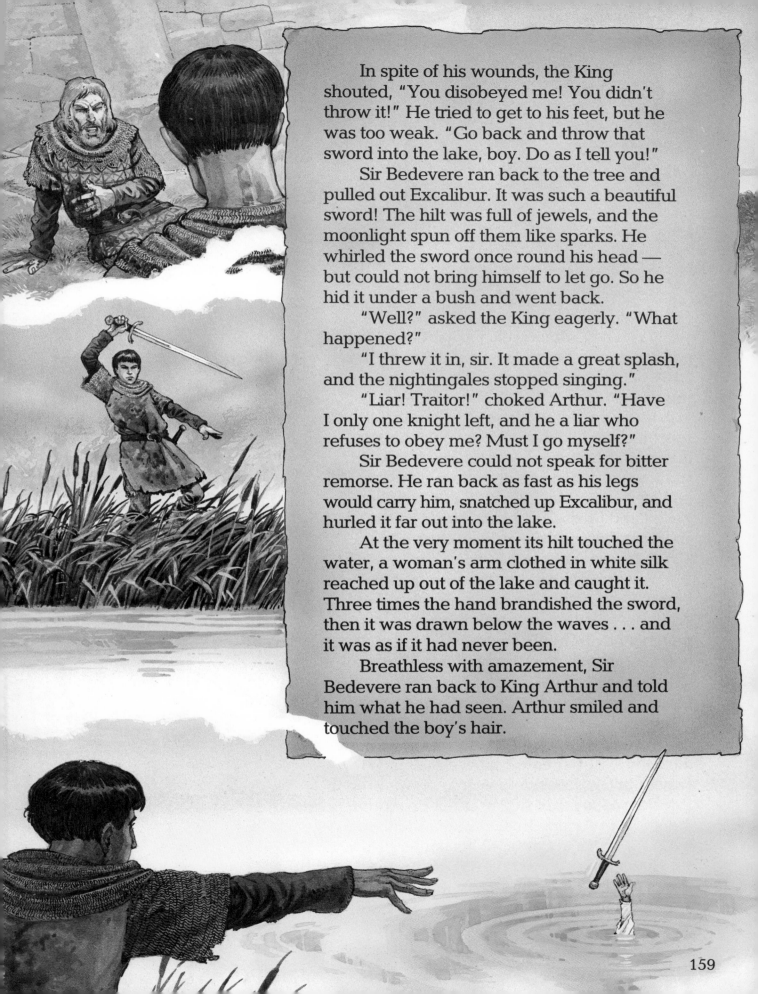

In spite of his wounds, the King shouted, "You disobeyed me! You didn't throw it!" He tried to get to his feet, but he was too weak. "Go back and throw that sword into the lake, boy. Do as I tell you!"

Sir Bedevere ran back to the tree and pulled out Excalibur. It was such a beautiful sword! The hilt was full of jewels, and the moonlight spun off them like sparks. He whirled the sword once round his head — but could not bring himself to let go. So he hid it under a bush and went back.

"Well?" asked the King eagerly. "What happened?"

"I threw it in, sir. It made a great splash, and the nightingales stopped singing."

"Liar! Traitor!" choked Arthur. "Have I only one knight left, and he a liar who refuses to obey me? Must I go myself?"

Sir Bedevere could not speak for bitter remorse. He ran back as fast as his legs would carry him, snatched up Excalibur, and hurled it far out into the lake.

At the very moment its hilt touched the water, a woman's arm clothed in white silk reached up out of the lake and caught it. Three times the hand brandished the sword, then it was drawn below the waves . . . and it was as if it had never been.

Breathless with amazement, Sir Bedevere ran back to King Arthur and told him what he had seen. Arthur smiled and touched the boy's hair.

"You have done well. Excalibur was not mine, you see. It was only lent to me by the Lady of the Lake. Now carry me down to the shore."

Bedevere lifted him one last time, but reaching the lake found it no longer deserted. Moored among the reeds was a shallow barge draped at bow, masthead and stern with black cloth. Three women, veiled and dressed in black, stood on the shore beckoning. "Lay him in the boat, Sir Bedevere. Your task is finished."

Wrapped in rugs, in the bow of the barge, King Arthur seemed to be sleeping. As Bedevere stepped out of the barge, it pulled away from the shore and into the heart of the lake where mists draped it round.

"Where are you taking him?" Bedevere called across the water. And the answer came back, "To Avalon! To Avalon!"

And that was the last any mortal saw of the King — the greatest knight ever to wear armour, the greatest hero ever to draw sword.

People say that Arthur is not dead: that the herbs of Avalon healed him and he is sleeping, worn out after all his battles. They say that if the country is in danger and needs its best warriors, Arthur and his fallen knights may come back some day from the magic vale called Avalon.